SEW DEADLY

An Iris House B&B Mystery

JEAN HAGER

G.K. Hall & Co. • Chivers Press
Waterville, Maine USA   Bath, England

This Large Print edition is published by G.K. Hall & Co., USA and by Chivers Press, England.

Published in 2001 in the U.S. by arrangement with Avon Books, an imprint of HarperCollins Publishers, Inc.

Published in 2001 in the U.K. by arrangement with The Author.

U.S. Softcover 0-7838-9498-8 (Paperback Series Edition)
U.K. Hardcover 0-7540-4587-0 (Chivers Large Print)
U.K. Softcover 0-7540-4588-9 (Camden Large Print)

This is a work of fiction. Names, characters, places, and incidents either are the products of the author's imagination or are used fictitiously. Any resemblance to actual events, locales, organizations, or persons, living or dead, is entirely coincidental.

The text of this Large Print Edition is unabridged.
Other aspects of the book may vary from the original edition.

Set in 16 pt. Plantin.

Printed in the United States on permanent paper.

British Library Cataloguing in Publication Data available

Library of Congress Cataloging-in-Publication Data

Hager, Jean.
Sew deadly : an Iris House B&B mystery / Jean Hager.
p. cm.
ISBN 0-7838-9498-8 (lg. print : sc : alk. paper)
1. Darcy, Tess (Fictitious character) — Fiction. 2. Iris House (Victoria Springs, Mo. : Imaginary place) — Fiction. 3. Bed and breakfast accommodations — Fiction. 4. Women detectives — Missouri — Fiction. 5. Large type books. I. Title.
PS3558.A3232 S49 2001
813′.54—dc21 2001024443

This book is dedicated to Art Dellin,
who paid good money to get
Ross's name in print.

1

"I'm going to kill her!" Ross Dellin shouted as he barreled into the room. Three women who stood in the doorway scattered like trespassing children fleeing a charging bull.

Regulars at the senior citizens center were accustomed to Ross's bovine method of locomotion, head thrust forward as though he were looking for something to butt out of his way, bushy white eyebrows bristling. But murder threats were a bit over the top, even for Ross.

He lumbered to a halt and swept a scathing gaze over the five people already gathered for the book discussion group, finally fixing his eyes on Tess Darcy, who stood in the circle of chairs, chatting with her cousin Cinny Forrest. Cinny, owner of the Queen Street Book Shop, organized the weekly book discussions at the center and provided discounted paperback editions of books chosen by the group.

Pretending not to notice that Ross had homed in on her and was stomping her way, Tess tried to focus on Cinny's lament that she might as well have closed the bookshop during

January and February for all the business she'd done.

Regardless of the lull in the book business, Tess had fully expected to start the book discussion herself, as Cinny was usually late for everything. Her arrival ten minutes before the appointed time made Tess wonder if her cousin, now a small business owner, might be mending her ways. More likely, Cinny was just bored being in the shop with no customers.

As for Tess, she had no guest reservations for her Iris House Bed and Breakfast until the first of March, the beginning of Victoria Springs's tourist season. Gertie Bogart, the Iris House cook, had insisted on filling the freezer with breakfast items, in case unexpected guests moved in while Gertie was on vacation. Confident she could make do without Gertie if need be, Tess had focused her attention elsewhere during this down time and volunteered five or six hours a day at the senior citizens center for the month of February. So far, she'd mostly run errands for the director and shuttled seniors around town.

Much of the remainder of her days was spent mulling over how she and Luke Fredrik could establish a home together while she continued to run her bed and breakfast and he stayed in his house, where he had a suite of offices from which he and his assistant, Sidney Lawson, managed investment portfolios for several handpicked and very loyal clients. Tess and

Luke had become engaged right after Christmas, and Luke was pressing her to set a wedding date. Tess was reminded of this every time she noticed the large diamond solitaire on her third finger, left hand.

But at the moment, she had other problems to deal with. Mainly the contentious Ross Dellin, who was bearing down on her.

As he clomped to Tess's side, Ross's nostrils flared, and the fringed ends of the plaid wool scarf looped around his neck fluttered in the breeze generated by his passage. "Where is she?" he demanded loudly.

Tess faced him, narrowing her eyes in displeasure at his high-handed manner. "Who?"

"Edwina Riley," he roared. "She's done it again!"

"Done what, Ross?"

"Filched my locker! Moved my stuff" — he waved a copy of the mystery novel they would be discussing that morning under Tess's nose — "to the top row and installed her things in *my* box."

Cubbyholes were provided for seniors who wanted to leave books, games or sewing supplies at the center rather than cart them back and forth. The lockers, as they were called, weren't assigned and could be used on a first come, first served basis. In theory, if you found one empty, you could claim it. But everybody knew that Ross was partial to the first locker in the bottom row, and all were content to steer clear of that space, even when it was empty.

All except Edwina, who was not known for avoiding confrontations. In fact, Tess suspected she enjoyed them. Edwina was short, barely five feet tall, and couldn't reach the upper rows. Several times lately, she'd complained that all the lockers in the lower rows were taken and that taller people — like Ross, a six-foot, barrel-chested man in his early seventies who tipped the scale at close to two hundred pounds — should be considerate enough to leave them for shorties like her.

Ross didn't see it that way, and he'd informed Edwina huffily that he'd gotten there first and had no intention of giving up his locker. On three previous occasions, Edwina, apparently using a chair to stand on, had transferred Ross's belongings to one of the upper rows and installed her own things in the first locker in the bottom row. It now appeared she'd done it again, probably yesterday after Ross had left the center. Edwina could be as bullheaded as Ross. She was just sneakier about it. The two habitually fussed and argued like cranky children. Sadly, at their ages, putting them down for naps and expecting them to wake up in a better mood wasn't an option.

"I haven't seen Edwina this morning," Tess replied to Ross's question.

"I'm sure she'll be here," Cinny put in. "We're discussing the cozy mystery she campaigned for." At the previous meeting of the book group, Edwina and Ross had engaged in a heated argument over the merits, or lack thereof, of cozies versus hard-boiled mysteries. Ross, of course, was a hard-boiled fan.

He glared at the paperback book clutched in his beefy hand, and his upper lip curled in contempt. On the cover was a yellow house whose bay window revealed a white cat napping next to a teapot on a pink-draped table. "Ridiculous fluff!" he snorted.

"That's but one opinion," Tess told him. "And you're entitled to it. Just don't try to force it on everyone else."

He frowned at her, then returned to his first complaint. "I'm going to the office now to get some adhesive tape that I can use to stick my name on *my* locker." John L. Lewis eyebrows lowered over grim dark eyes which dared Tess to tell him that labeling the lockers was against the rules. When Tess refused to play his game, he turned on his heel, lowered his head, and plowed back across the room and down the hall toward the office. Tess had no thought of trying to stop him. Let Jennifer Vercourt, the center's director, deal with the contentious Ross Dellin.

"I'm surprised Edwina isn't here by now," Cinny said, glancing at her watch with irritation. Tapping one boot-clad foot, she tucked a strand of long blond hair behind a small, pearl-studded ear. "We're supposed to start in five minutes." The perennially tardy Cinny became impatient when she was the one doing the waiting.

"I called her last night," Tess said, "to see if she needed transportation to the center this morning." Edwina didn't own a car because, she said, she couldn't afford to keep it up. "Her nephew's bringing her. He's visiting from Texas."

"I'll try calling her again," Cinny said and hurried from the room. "If she has company, she may have lost track of the time."

The three women whom Ross had nearly trampled underfoot when he made his entrance — Joyce Banaker, Mercy Bates, and Anita McBroom — drifted over to the circle of chairs.

Joyce, clutching her mystery novel in both hands, chose a chair with deliberation. Mercy took a seat next to her, using one beringed hand to smooth her tightly permed cap of dyed black hair, a startling contrast to her lined and sagging face. Mercy did her best to camouflage her age with much rouge and lipstick. Sadly, Tess thought, Mercy only succeeded in looking garish. The many large costume rings she wore, most of them acquired at garage sales, didn't help, either.

Mercy lived in one of the center's ten apartments. Since the apartments qualified as low-income housing, the government helped pay the rent of the seniors who lived there.

"Joyce," Mercy said, "maybe Edwina will take advantage of her nephew's visit and get him to paint her house."

Joyce, still spry at eighty, rolled her shrewd brown eyes. "I should be so lucky, but I don't think it'll happen. Edwina says she can't afford to do anything to her property." Tall and thin, Joyce settled precisely erect in her chair, her feet in comfortable black lace-ups planted flat on the floor. "Which is probably true at this point. She should have taken care of repairs as they became necessary."

Mercy bobbed her head. "Well, she only has her social security check to live on — like me."

"I understand that, but the house is going to fall down on top of her if she doesn't do something soon," Joyce said. "This last year, the place has gone to rack and ruin. Every time I look out my bedroom window, I get so mad I could bite nails. Edwina's property is a blight on the neighborhood."

Tess, who'd been listening with interest, walked over to join the conversation. "I know how distressing it is to have a rundown property right next door," she commiserated with Joyce.

"Albert used to help her out with repairs," Anita said, "but since his back surgery, he hasn't been able." Anita, whose most vocal regret was that she no longer had the lush and lovely red hair of her youth, touched her gray bangs with her fingertips. Somehow, though, Tess suspected that wasn't Anita's only regret; she just didn't talk about the others. But sometimes Tess caught her staring into space, the most disconsolate expression on her face.

Like Mercy, Anita lived in an apartment attached to the center. Her husband, Albert, a retired public school principal, wasn't a reader of fiction and didn't take part in the book discussions. Anita sat down at Joyce's other side. "Joyce, didn't I hear that you offered to buy the paint for the exterior of Edwina's house?"

Joyce removed a loose hairpin from her gray French knot and stabbed it back into place. "I certainly did! Though Lord knows I have all I can manage keeping my own place up." A retired science teacher who'd spent her working life dealing with rambunctious teenagers, Joyce was nothing if not direct.

Mercy's eyes grew wide as she laid a hand along her rouged cheek and giggled. "Knowing Edwina, I don't expect she took that very well." Mercy and Edwina Riley had been high school classmates in the '40s.

Joyce gave a sniff of vexation. "She was already miffed by the petition the neighbors presented to her, asking her to fix her place up. She blames me for starting it, but I swear it wasn't my idea. I did sign it, of course. Then I went over and said I'd buy the paint, thinking it would soften the effect of the petition. She got snippy and said my offer was adding insult to injury. Asked if I was volunteering my labor, too, as she wasn't about to start climbing around on ladders at her age."

Irritation flashed in Anita's hazel eyes. "What a nerve that woman has! Why, you're older than Edwina."

"By several years," Joyce said. Unlike Mercy, Joyce never tried to shave a few years off her age. "Edwina knew very well I had no intention of doing the painting. She was just putting me in my place."

Mercy nodded knowingly. "She's good at that."

"Now," Joyce went on, "she refuses to ride to the center with the traitor, as she calls me. She'd rather ask somebody else to go out of their way to pick her up." She glanced at Tess. "Like Tess here."

"Oh, I don't mind," Tess said, "as long as I'm coming anyway."

Mercy shook her head. Her jet curls jiggled. "Edwina can be such a trial." She leaned closer to Joyce and added in hushed tones, "I wouldn't want it to get back to Edwina that I'd said this, but — well, I'd watch out for her if I were you, dear. Edwina holds a grudge forever, and she can do some really mean things when you get on her bad side."

"Don't I know it," Joyce agreed. "Lately she's taken to looking for some infraction of city ordinances over at my place so she can report me."

"Edwina has reported *you?*" Tess asked disbelievingly. There wasn't a neater house in town than Joyce's bungalow, and her yard was always well maintained.

"Oh, yes. Three times," Joyce said. "Most recently that weekend last month when I went out of town. You know city regulations stipulate that you should set your trash at the curb for the refuse truck no more than twenty-four hours prior to the scheduled pickup. Since I was going to be gone, I put my trash out forty-eight hours ahead of time. When I got home, I had a reminder from the city stuck in my screen door. I was sorely tempted to go straight to Edwina and give her a piece of my mind."

"It wouldn't have done any good," Mercy told her, pursing her red-glossed lips. "In fact, it would probably have made matters worse." She spoke as if she had learned this from long experience.

"I know, and that's why I didn't do it. But I did make a point of telling her that my husband's old Mustang would be parked in the street in front of my house this week while I'm having the garage foundation worked on. Just so she'd know." Tess had heard Joyce say once that she couldn't bear to part with the vintage Mustang because her late husband had loved it so much. She washed and polished it regularly and kept it running by taking it out for a short drive every week. Otherwise, the car was stored in a detached garage behind Joyce's house. Tess had seen the car, which appeared to be in perfect condition, and guessed it would bring a good amount of money from a collector if Joyce ever decided to sell it.

Anita made a clicking sound with her tongue. "You'd think the city inspector would notice the condition of Edwina's house while he's leaving you those reminders."

Joyce shrugged. "Perhaps peeling paint and rotting fences aren't infractions of city rules."

"Even if the inspector suggested to Edwina that she do something about her property," Anita added, "she'd just promise to take care of things right away. Of course, she'd do no such thing."

Mercy sighed in acknowledgment, then glanced toward the door and beamed. "Oh, here comes Wally."

A slim man of about Mercy's age, with a salt-and-pepper toothbrush moustache and wearing brown corduroy trousers and a green flannel shirt, made his way toward the circle.

"Oh, good," Tess said. "Some new blood for the group."

Suddenly animated and slightly flustered, Mercy jumped up and met Wally in the middle of the circle. "Tess, Joyce, Anita," she said, "this is my friend Wally Tanksley. I invited him to join our book discussion."

Greetings were exchanged, and Mercy led Wally a little away from the other women. They sat side by side and immediately began a conversation in low tones, their heads bent toward each other.

Joyce looked at Tess and lifted an eyebrow.

"Well, well. Mercy's got a boyfriend," she whispered.

"It would seem so."

"That must be the man she mentioned to me the other day," Anita said. "She met him at church." Anita glanced toward the door. "Here come the rest of our group, and still no Edwina."

Seventy-five-year-old twins, Opal and Hattie Bloom (their late husbands had been brothers), and Don Bob Earling, a frail, elderly man with a beard and a cane, greeted the others and were introduced to Mercy's friend as they found chairs. Don Bob was one of the people who played dominoes or cards many weekday afternoons at the center. A fierce competitor, he had from time to time accused both Ross and Edwina of cheating, accusations both had heatedly denied.

Just then, Ross stormed back into the room with a triumphant look on his face and took his place in the circle.

Cinny, who for the last few minutes had been pacing impatiently near the door, consulted her watch again. She returned to the circle of chairs and sat down. "Edwina didn't answer her phone, so she must be on the way. We'll give her another couple of minutes before we start."

"Hmmph!" Ross growled. "Don't know why we can't start on time. People who can't be punctual shouldn't expect the rest of us to cool our heels till they can bestir their lazy bones to get here."

Mercy, her hand draped through the crook of Wally's elbow, giggled. "Edwina may be a lot of things, but I never thought lazy was one of them."

"Evidently, Mercy, you have never been inside her house," Joyce commented. "It's filthy!"

Mercy waved a hand, almost dislodging a ring with a huge, green glass stone. "Actually, I have. You certainly couldn't call it neat, the way every corner's crammed full of junk, but that doesn't make it dirty."

Tess wondered why Mercy felt called upon to defend Edwina, whose barbed jibes had hit Mercy as often as anybody else.

As for Edwina's house, Tess had been inside, and it wasn't only the corners that were crammed full of junk. In the living room, the only room Tess had seen, there was a narrow path, covered with ancient packed-down shag carpeting of indeterminate hue, leading to the hall, off which the kitchen and bedrooms opened. Stacks of magazines, newspapers and assorted litter — totally useless litter as far as Tess could tell — filled the rest of the room. Tess would bet that the other rooms were similarly packed. Edwina was one of those people who couldn't bring herself to part with anything from a snippet of twine to a piece of junk mail.

Tess was certain Edwina rarely, if ever, moved her accumulated belongings to clean, a herculean task that would have taken an able-bodied crew several days to accomplish. Besides, there was no other place for Edwina or a crew of workers to move it to.

"It's an illness, you know, a compulsion to keep everything that comes into one's hands," Mercy was saying. "So you can't really blame Edwina. She can't help it."

Tess thought Mercy was merely trying to make excuses for Edwina. For what reason Tess didn't know, unless it was that Mercy wanted to be liked by everyone, even the often quarrelsome Edwina. Or maybe Mercy, with a new boyfriend to show off, was just feeling magnanimous.

With a flourish, Ross opened his book to a turned-down page. "Don't know about the rest of you, but I've got better things to do than wait on Edwina," he announced. "Let's get this show on the road. I'll start by saying that the whole premise of this thing is totally unbelievable."

"You can't make unsubstantiated statements like that!" Joyce stated, reaching for her own copy. "You have to back up your opinion with evidence from the book. That's the rule."

"You want evidence?" Ross demanded. "I'll give you evidence. According to the list of book titles in the front of this piece of shit" — he waved the book in the air — "this is the fourth in a series. How —"

As usual, Ross's language caused Anita McBroom to scowl with distaste and the Bloom sisters to press their lips together in two disapproving lines.

"As civilized people, we should be able to have a discussion without resorting to the language of street thugs," Anita snapped, tugging at her gray bangs.

"That's right, Ross," Opal Bloom chimed in. "If you'll remember, profanity is against the rules, too."

Don Bob sat forward, one hand resting on the crook of his cane. "Don't we all know by now," he muttered, "that Ross doesn't think rules apply to him?"

Ross scowled at him and then the three women. "What a bunch of namby-pambies!"

Tess and Cinny exchanged a glance. It appeared they were going to begin without Edwina.

"Nevertheless, Ross," Cinny put in, attempting to take charge, "you know that kind of language is offensive to some members of the group, so please cut it out."

Ross's glance slid over Cinny as if he were taking notice of a faintly pesky gnat. Then he sent a belligerent look around the circle. "As I was saying before I was so rudely interrupted, how many librarians do you know who stumble over one body in a lifetime, much less four? Furthermore," he continued, undaunted, "the cops would never tolerate some old-maid librarian interfering in a police investigation."

"We've already covered that territory," Tess reminded him. "When we chose this book, one of the guidelines we agreed upon was that with amateur-sleuth novels you must be willing to suspend disbelief on that particular point."

"Maybe the rest of you agreed upon it," Ross blustered, "but I can't delude myself so easily. That's why I read realistic mysteries. Give me Robert B. Parker or John D. MacDonald any day!"

"Your assumption that those books are realistic is flawed to begin with," said Joyce authoritatively, sounding like the schoolteacher she had been. "I belong to a writers group that meets at the library, and last month we had a real private investigator speak to us. She said her life was nothing like what you read in private-eye novels."

"Horse hockey!" Ross bleated. "Your speaker was a female."

"What's your point, Ross?" Joyce demanded.

"That's who reads these amateur-sleuth books — women who are too squeamish to deal with true-to-life crime."

"Even if that were true," Joyce returned, "it doesn't negate what that private investigator told us about her work, which I'm sure she knows more about than you do, Ross. Besides, reading a crime novel of any kind is not dealing with actual crime."

Don Bob interrupted. "If people want real crime, they'll watch the news. They read fiction to escape reality for a while. Personally, I like amateur-sleuth books. They're some of the best whodunits being written today. A lot of men read them."

Ross raked the older man with a caustic look. "I'm talking about *real* men, Don Bob."

This wasn't the first time Ross had said something to Don Bob that made Tess wonder if the older man was gay. She knew he had never married, which in itself was probably enough to make someone like Ross, who'd outlived two wives, suspicious of his sexual orientation.

Wally Tanksley cleared his throat. "I'm new to the group," he said hesitantly, "and maybe I shouldn't speak up so soon, and I haven't read this particular book, of course, but as a rule I enjoy amateur-sleuth novels, too."

"And nobody could say that Wally isn't a real man," Mercy simpered, peering over at Wally admiringly. Modestly Wally ducked his head.

Ross gazed steadily at Wally, sizing him up, then evidently decided he was an irritant best ignored.

Don Bob's face above his beard had flushed a deep red, and he'd laid his book on the floor to grip the curve of his cane with both hands. He put so much weight on the cane that the tip slipped and the cane clattered to the floor. Don Bob let it lie. "What would you know about being a real anything, Ross, except maybe a stinking horse's patoot!"

Ross glowered at the agitated older man. "Listen here, you prissy old fag —"

"That's it! I've had it with you, Ross!" Don Bob reached for his cane, his face flushed even redder than before, so that Tess feared he was about to have a stroke. Troubled, she watched him scrabble for the cane and wondered if he meant to hit Ross with it.

"Oh, yeah?" Ross retorted. "The truth hurts, doesn't it? So what're you gonna do about it?"

Don Bob had finally grasped the cane. He flailed it in Ross's direction, "You bastard —"

"Don Bob!" cried Anita and clapped her hands over her ears.

Opal Bloom gasped, and Hattie shook her head. "So, Ross," Hattie inserted into the growing furor, "are you saying that Parker's and MacDonald's books are true to-life?"

Distracted, Ross turned toward Hattie. "Absolutely!"

Don Bob had come half out of his seat, leaning on his cane. For a long moment, he crouched there, vacillating, then seemed to think better of getting up. Lowering himself back into his chair with a grunt, he propped his cane against his knee and picked up his book. Tess was relieved to see that he appeared less flushed. Then he scratched his chin through his beard and snorted. "That's a load of crap."

Cinny shook a finger at Don Bob. "Language, Don Bob," she reminded him. "If you and Ross can't be civil, you aren't welcome here."

Both men glowered at Cinny. It was Ross who finally spoke, but not to apologize. As far as Tess knew, apologies weren't part of Ross's repertoire.

"The point I was trying to make is that Parker and MacDonald deal with the grit and grime of human existence," Ross said.

Several female voices rose to disagree with Ross, while Ross and Don Bob tried to stare each other down.

Cinny stood and shouted that the women were breaking yet another rule, the one that said they should lift a hand and wait to be recognized before speaking.

2

Milly Juniper covered a big yawn with her left hand, the one sporting the fake gold wedding band Skip had insisted she wear while in Victoria Springs. With a bored sigh, she stared at the back of Edwina Riley's gray head, at the tight little bun that looked like a weather-whitened dog turd with a hundred hairpins sticking in it.

Milly had hardly slept at all last night on that pitiful excuse for a bed, and then Skip had insisted that she get up and go with him to take Edwina to the senior citizens center. This while Edwina stood outside the closed bedroom door, babbling, "Oh me, oh my, we're going to be late if Milly doesn't get a move on."

At one point, Edwina had said to Skip that she hoped Milly wasn't going to be one of those wives who slept till noon. She'd said it loudly enough for Milly to hear through the door, because of course the remark had really been meant for Milly.

Milly had wanted to shout at Edwina that she couldn't afford to sleep till noon because *somebody* had to go to work on a regular basis if she and Skip were to eat. Milly had known this woman less than twenty-four hours and already she heartily disliked her.

She had finally given up trying to sleep and crawled out of bed. She hadn't unpacked her suitcase, so she dressed in the jeans and sweater she'd taken off the night before.

But not quickly enough to suit Edwina, who'd mumbled that the book discussion was surely going on that very minute without her.

Major catastrophe, Milly had griped to herself. *The collapse of western civilization as we know it.*

Then, as Milly emerged from the bedroom, Edwina had announced that she'd just remembered something. She had to make a phone call before they left. Milly suspected she'd done that on purpose, too, just to irritate Milly further. Nobody said anything about breakfast. Milly assumed that Edwina and Skip had already eaten.

Finally they were ready to go. Skip, of course, had insisted that his Aunt Edwina take the front passenger seat and leave the back seat of Milly's Honda for Milly. They'd brought her car because it was more dependable than Skip's old Chevy.

As they drove away from Edwina's dilapidated house, Milly had asked herself for at least the dozenth time what she was doing there. Why had she ever said she'd be a partner in this sham honeymoon from hell? It was another of Skip's absurd brainstorms, and she couldn't believe she'd agreed to it.

Skip had urgently wanted to pay a visit to Edwina, but he hadn't wanted to go without Milly. So he'd phoned his aunt last week to tell her that he and Milly had gotten married and wanted to share their happiness with her by coming for a visit. Listening to him, Milly would have believed him herself if she hadn't known better. Skip was a world-class liar. Of course, with gullible old Edwina it was like taking candy from a baby.

Edwina, who, according to Skip, had been hinting for some time that Skip needed to settle down, had been delighted over the impending visit. To prepare for the newlyweds' arrival, she had moved about a ton of stuff off the lumpy mattress in her spare room to uncover the marriage bed. She'd stacked the displaced debris on top of piles of other rubbish lining the walls. With the additional junk, the stacks were so high that they teetered precariously when you got in bed. Milly had refused to have sex last night because she feared the activity would dislodge something and the whole roomful of trash would collapse and suffocate them.

Besides, she wasn't in a romantic mood. She was really ticked off at Skip. He should have warned her about Edwina's house. He hadn't, of course, because he knew she'd never have come. If only she hadn't let Skip's pleading wear her down. When, upon their arrival last night, she had realized the horror of her situation, it had been too late to make other arrangements.

Now, God help her, she was on her way to the old folks center.

Slumped in the rear seat, staring at the back of Edwina's head, Milly made a decision. She would not spend another night in that bed or pass her days listening to Edwina's boring conversation. As soon as she could get Skip alone, she was going to tell him. She'd find a motel room. Skip could go with her or stay with Auntie, as he chose.

The trip to Victoria Springs was necessary, Skip had explained to Milly, because Aunt Edwina was getting old. She had already had a little flare-up with her heart; she practically had one foot in the grave already, and could drop dead at any time. He didn't want her to think he was neglecting her, and it was essential that she get to know Milly.

Implied in the message was that Milly should knock herself out to charm the old lady. Having met Edwina, Milly didn't think she was charmable. The lie about the marriage was necessary, too, Skip said, because Aunt Edwina was kind of strait-laced, and he was pretty sure she would not tolerate their sharing a bed in her house prior to the knot being tied. Edwina thought they had separate apartments in Fort Worth. If she knew they'd been living together for almost a year, Skip said, she might write him out of her will, even if he was her dead sister's boy and her only living relative.

Big, hairy deal, Milly had thought when she'd seen the hovel that Edwina called home. Clearly Auntie didn't have a pot to pee in. They hadn't been in the house five minutes before Edwina cautioned them not to use too much toilet tissue and to turn off the lights when they left a room. Last evening, when Milly announced her intention to take a bath, Edwina had handed her a threadbare towel and washcloth with the advice that two inches of water in the tub was plenty for a good scrub. Clearly Edwina had to pinch every penny.

But Skip, who inhabited a fantasy world half the time, still insisted that you couldn't judge by appearances. His aunt had not taken another husband after a brief marriage in her early years but had reclaimed her maiden name and lived alone, working as a secretary-receptionist for a local insurance office until she was seventy. Milly was sure Edwina's salary had probably provided only bare subsistence — after all, would she live in that house if she could afford better?

From a couple of things Edwina had said, Milly surmised that the old woman didn't have a pension from her former employer but lived solely on her social security check now. How could Skip believe she'd managed to put anything away? But that was Skip for you. Don't confuse him with the facts. He persisted in his opinion that you never could tell about old people, and the family had always joked about how frugal Edwina was, which Milly now realized must be the understatement of the century. Surely, Skip had said, Edwina had managed to tuck away a few thousand. Last night after they'd gone to bed, he'd speculated that Edwina could have five or ten thousand in the bank, adding, "And this house must be worth something."

Milly had laughed so hard she'd almost choked. "You couldn't give away this rat's nest."

"We'd clean it up first," Skip had said.

To which Milly had replied, "Speak for yourself, Skip. But if you remove all those stacks of trash, the walls will collapse. That's the only thing holding them up."

"Don't be so negative," Skip had countered. "We could get a few thousand out of the house. The lot alone has to be worth something. With that and whatever she's got in the bank, we could really get married."

Skip, the eternal optimist. Every time he sent off one of those sweepstakes entries that came in the mail, he expected to win, and he'd spend hours daydreaming about what he'd buy with the money.

Recently Skip had had plenty of time to daydream, since he was between jobs, a situation that was getting to be a habit with him. Sure, the guy was cute, with his freckles and lopsided, little-boy grin, but during the past year,

Skip's fatal flaw had become all too clear to Milly. He couldn't seem to stick with a job for more than a few months before getting restless. That other employees had it in for him was the usual excuse.

When Skip wasn't working, they lived on Milly's salary as a computer programmer. And lately she'd begun to suspect that Skip wasn't looking very hard for another job. Milly was having serious second thoughts about ever marrying him.

"When we get to the center," Edwina was saying, "I want to introduce you to my book discussion group, Skippy. Then you and Milly can go and come back for me later. Or you can watch TV in the rec room until lunch time." She twisted around to look at Milly. "Jenny always serves a nice hot noonday meal. At a very reasonable price, too."

"Marvelous," Milly mumbled, only half-attending to what Edwina was saying.

"If you pay for lunches by the month," Edwina went on, "you get a discount. Even those of us who don't live at the center eat a lot of lunches there. It's actually cheaper than fixing the same thing at home, if you can believe it. Except for last-minute lunches. They cost more — five dollars a person."

Must be bologna sandwiches and Jell-O, Milly thought. *Terrific.*

Skip reached over and patted Edwina's blue-veined hand. "Lunch sounds like fun, Auntie.

Don't you think so, Milly?"

What Milly thought was that if the center had a vending machine, she might just make it till dinner time, which she planned to eat out — alone, if Skip refused to join her. "Yeah," she said.

"Oh, good. I'll tell Jenny you'll stay then."

"Okay, but I won't have you buying our lunch, Aunt Edwina," Skip said magnanimously, although Milly hadn't heard her offer. "You've already had to buy extra groceries for our visit. We'll pay for our lunch."

You mean I'll pay, Mr. Big Bucks, Milly fumed silently.

"Well, all right, if you insist, Skippy," Edwina said.

"I do, Aunt Edwina."

"You are such a thoughtful boy. Isn't he something, Milly?"

"He's incredible."

"It's so sweet of you, Skippy, to understand that I have to economize to make my social security check last a month. Everything costs so much these days. And as you say, my grocery bill will be higher this week. Not that I begrudge it. I do so love having you here, Skippy."

Skip gave his aunt that mischievous little-boy grin. "And I love being here, too. It's been way too long since I saw you — have to keep the old nose to the grindstone, you know, now that I've got a family to support — but I've missed you, Aunt Edwina."

Milly stifled a groan. *I can't stand a full week of this,* she told herself. *I really can't.*

"That's it," Edwina chirped, and for an instant Milly thought the old bag wasn't fooled by Skip's lies, but then she realized that Edwina was pointing at a sprawling white building on their right. A sign in the yard said: SENIOR CITIZENS CENTER. Nothing fancy about the place, but it looked roomy. "You can park on the west side," Edwina said, gesturing for Skippy to turn in. "I love this place. It's my home away from home. I honestly don't know what I'd do with myself if I couldn't come to the center."

How about cleaning house? Milly thought. She hadn't seen the inside of the center yet, but she figured it had to beat that dump Edwina lived in six ways from Sunday.

Skip parked in the graveled lot beside the center, then ran around to help Edwina out of the car. Skippy in the role of thoughtful nephew and gallant gentleman continued to amaze Milly as she struggled out of the back seat on her own and trailed Skip and Edwina to the door of the center. She wished she knew exactly what was going on in Skip's mind.

"We have quilting circle after lunch," Edwina was saying. "We're working on a Tumbling Blocks pattern for the Methodist minister's wife." She turned to see if Milly was keeping up. "We get paid, too, Milly."

"Wow," Milly said.

Edwina prattled on, plainly not recognizing sarcasm when she heard it. "The center takes twenty percent, and by the time we split up the rest, we only earn fifteen or twenty dollars a quilt. But every little bit helps, you know." Again she twisted her head around and almost caught Milly sticking out her tongue. "Do you quilt, Milly, dear?"

"Er . . . no, ma'am."

"What a shame. You don't know what you're missing."

"I never had time to learn, I guess," said Milly, whose skill with a needle consisted of reattaching buttons that fell off her clothes.

"Your mother doesn't quilt, then?"

"No."

"Well, I'll teach you. Oh, my, I do love to quilt." Edwina waved both hands in the air. "I've got scars on my fingers from it. I simply can't use a thimble, it feels too awkward. I'm always pricking my fingers, but I'm used to it." She paused as if expecting some response from Milly, perhaps congratulations on her dedication to quilting in spite of bloody fingers.

"Uh-huh," Milly said.

"I also crochet, Milly. I buy cast-off doilies and tablecloths at garage sales and unravel them for the thread. Sometimes people will just give you that stuff to get you to take it away. I'll teach you crocheting, too."

When pigs fly, Milly thought. "Can't wait," she said, trying not to grind her teeth.

"You can sit in on our sewing circle today if you want to."

"Er . . . I may have to run to town for a few toiletries."

"Another time, then. You know, Skippy, most young girls nowadays have no interest at all in the domestic arts. You made a good choice in a wife, dear."

"Don't I know it, Auntie."

They had reached the center's entrance. Skip opened the door and stood back for Edwina and Milly to pass through. Milly quirked an eyebrow at him. She couldn't remember the last time he'd opened a door for her at home.

She followed Edwina into a large room with black and white linoleum tiles on the floor. The room, which was spotlessly clean and smelled of lemon-scented polish, was furnished with several mismatched but comfortable-looking couches and chairs. A large-screen TV set took up one corner, and there was a pool table against the wall. Plain and serviceable but, next to Edwina's house, it was a mansion.

"This is the rec room," Edwina said. They draped their coats on a rack which was already covered with other coats. "Isn't it wonderful?" Edwina asked, beaming, as she watched Skip and Milly expectantly for their response. *What did she expect? Gasps of awe, perhaps.*

"This is nice," Skip said. "Isn't it, Milly?"

"Yeah, charming."

"There's usually somebody watching TV, but

I guess they're all busy elsewhere right now. Sometimes Jenny rents a video and some of us watch a movie after lunch. There're usually a few people playing pool at the same time. You might want to try it, Skippy."

"Sure."

"Otherwise," Edwina rattled on, "when we finish quilting, most of us play cards or dominoes in the game room behind the cafeteria. There's always something going on around here."

"Never a dull moment, huh?" Skip said.

A laugh a minute, Milly muttered to herself.

Edwina patted his hand. "That's right. Why, last month we had a birthday party for several of our regulars who have birthdays in January. Jenny found a magician to entertain us. I swear, I don't know how he did some of those tricks." She paused, as if to ponder the puzzle. Then she said, "Come with me. I'll get my book from my locker." She walked into a wide hallway tiled with the same black and white squares as the rec room, came to a dead halt, and let out a blood-curdling scream.

3

At the sound of a piercing wail, Tess and Cinny ran into the hallway. They were followed by the other members of the book discussion group. Jenny Vercourt, director and, with her husband, owner of the center, came running out of the kitchen. "What happened?"

Edwina Riley, in a much-laundered pink polyester pantsuit, stood next to the bank of lockers, wringing her hands. A sewing box and a hard-cover copy of the mystery novel the group had been discussing lay at her feet. Edwina got the books they discussed from the library, if possible. She said she couldn't afford even the discounted paperbacks that Cinny provided. When Edwina couldn't borrow the book, Cinny gave her one at no cost.

"That man threw my things on the floor!" Edwina shrieked. "Aha!" She reached out and ripped a piece of white adhesive tape bearing Ross Dellin's name off the front of the first locker in the bottom row. "Look at this! He's put his name on my locker!"

Ross lumbered forward. "That's *my* locker,

you crazy old witch! Keep your hands off it!" He moved to stand in front of the space in question and faced Edwina with his arms crossed over his chest.

The young man with Edwina put his arm around her. "Don't upset yourself, Auntie. I'm sure it's just a misunderstanding. We'll get it straightened out."

Ross's bristly brows scrunched together. "It's already straight, young man. So mind your own damn business!"

Tess noticed a weary-looking young woman with ash-blond hair standing behind Edwina and thought she saw the corners of her mouth trying to turn up. Whoever she was, she seemed to find the scene amusing.

Jenny, a fortyish woman, with wide gray eyes and a ready smile, wiped her hands on her apron and smoothed a falling strand of light-brown hair out of her eyes. "Now, Ross, you know you're not supposed to put your name on a locker."

"Well, she's not supposed to take my things out and put her own in, either."

Jenny looked at Edwina, who stamped her foot, which was clad in a scuffed, run-down brown oxford. "He took my things out first!" She waved a hand over the sewing box in the middle of the hall. "Now he's done it again, and I think he's trying to damage my belongings. There's the proof, and it's lucky the lid didn't come off. Besides, he knows I need one of the lockers on a lower row. I can't reach the top rows!"

"You're breaking my heart," Ross muttered, pretending to play an invisible violin. He dropped his arms. "News flash, Edwina. Your height is not my problem!"

"Make him move, Jenny," Edwina whined.

Ross glowered at Jenny and squared his shoulders as if to say lots of luck, you'll need a battering ram.

"Ross," Jenny said sternly, "I'm going to have to ask you to give up that locker."

Don Bob, looking quite pleased, smirked at Ross, clearly enjoying this put-down.

Ross's face flushed and his white eyebrows came together in a solid, bushy line as his frown grew more fierce. "For her? No way!"

"No, not for Edwina," Jenny said. "Albert's in the top row now, but he has trouble reaching so high because of his back. We'll make this his locker, and I want the two of you to keep your hands off it. Understood?"

Edwina sputtered, "But that's not fair!"

Jenny held up a hand. "End of discussion."

Ross growled, "What am I supposed to do with my things?"

"Stuff 'em up your —" Don Bob muttered. Tess didn't hear the rest of the suggestion, but could fill in the blank for herself.

"As Edwina says," Jenny told Ross, "you can easily reach the top row. Choose a locker there."

"What about me?" Edwina demanded, looking mulish.

Jenny's glance slid to one side, landing on the Bloom twins. "Opal and Hattie, can the two of you share a locker?"

The twins frowned, but finally Opal said grudgingly, "I suppose so."

"Good," Jenny said. "If you would move your things into Hattie's locker, Edwina can have yours. Now, is everybody satisfied?"

None of the parties involved looked particularly satisfied, but Ross removed his belongings and stashed them higher up, while Opal took her things from one of the lockers in the second row, which was still low enough for Edwina to reach.

That accomplished, Cinny said, "Shall we return to our book discussion?"

Elbowing past Edwina so roughly that she staggered back and had to reach for the wall to steady herself, Ross lumbered after the Bloom sisters into the meeting room. Tess watched him, thinking that his shoving Edwina had been no accident.

With clenched fists, Edwina righted herself and stared after Ross. "That man is just asking for it," she seethed. Then her gaze slid to Mercy and Wally as they walked away arm in arm. After a moment, she picked up her book and sewing box and put the box in Opal's former locker, clutching the book in one hand.

She introduced her nephew and his wife,

Skip and Milly Hector, to Jenny and Tess. "Jenny runs the center," Edwina explained, "and she deserves a medal for all she does for us. Tess is just helping out for a while. She owns a fancy bed and breakfast in town."

Skip, a good-looking young man with sandy hair and green eyes, gave them a brilliant smile while Edwina looked on with the pride of a mother whose child has just taken his first step. Milly offered a limp hand and mumbled a greeting.

Not a happy camper, Tess mused.

"Skip and Milly will be staying for lunch, Jenny," Edwina said. "Skippy, I don't want to interrupt the book discussion again. I'll introduce you to the others at lunch." She looked at Tess. "Who's the man with Mercy?"

"Wally something. He's a friend of Mercy's."

"Some poor, unsuspecting bachelor she's trying to hook, probably. Mercy is such a flirt." Edwina nodded her head emphatically, as if her pronouncement was above question. Then she scurried away to join the book discussion.

Into the fray, Tess thought. Plainly Edwina couldn't wait to come to loggerheads with Ross again. Mercy had said once that Edwina's greatest pleasure came from stirring up trouble, and Tess had come to agree with her.

The young couple headed for the rec room to watch TV, Milly muttering, "Oh, goody, maybe we can find some cartoons. Or how about a soap opera?"

"Come on, Milly," Skip mumbled. "Be a sport."

"I was out of my mind to let you drag me here," Milly said.

"Aw, Aunt Edwina's not so bad once you get to know her, honey. Just cut her some slack."

Tess couldn't hear Milly's reply, but she suspected Milly had already cut as much slack as she was going to.

Tess smiled at Jenny. "Do you ever feel like you're running a nursery school?"

"All the time," Jenny said with a laugh as she turned to go back to the kitchen.

Alone with Skip in the rec room, Milly was thinking that the trip to Victoria Springs was turning into a journey through Dante's nine circles of hell. First there was the pretend honeymoon hell and now geriatric hell. What next?

"I'm not spending another night in that house," Milly announced.

Skip gaped at her, horrified. "But we can't leave yet," he protested. "We haven't even been here twenty-four hours. If you'll just be patient a few days, I think I can get her to tell me how much she's leaving me. I'm going to tell her that we plan to name our first daughter after her."

"God, Skip, give me a break," Milly groaned.

"We won't actually do it, of course, but she'll be dead by the time we have a kid."

Milly glared at him in amazement. That old

woman would probably live to be a hundred.

"Come on, Milly. You can stand it for a few days." He lowered his voice. "Listen, I looked through her kitchen drawers last night and guess what I found."

"A mouse?"

"Very funny. No, I found an envelope from some place called Dillman and Haines, Investment and Trust Consultants. Aunt Edwina could have made some investments with them. The envelope was empty, so I couldn't find out for sure."

Milly snorted. "It was probably a solicitation, part of a blanket mailing. Investment firms do that all the time. Edwina must've used the back of the letter to make out a grocery list, then kept the envelope. You know she keeps everything."

Skip looked crestfallen. "Oh. Well, I guess that could be. Anyway, you can stay at Edwina's for another day or two, can't you?"

"Read my lips, Skip. No. We can stay somewhere else in town, and you can spend your days with Edwina. I'll entertain myself."

"You know I can't afford a motel."

"I'll put it on my credit card. If you're so afraid of hurting Edwina's feelings, you don't have to come with me. You can stay with your aunt and I'll find another place. Your choice, Skip."

"We're supposed to be on our honeymoon."

"Oh, good Lord, Skip! Why don't you just

tell the old biddy the truth?"

"No! She thinks I should settle down. You saw how pleased she is about the marriage."

"Don't you mean the big, fat lie you told her about the marriage?"

"Yeah, right." He pondered for a moment.

"Okay, then," Milly said, "if we're going to keep pretending we're on our honeymoon, we'll both spend our nights elsewhere. Edwina said that woman with the auburn hair — what's her name?"

"Tess Darcy?"

"Yeah. Edwina said she has a bed and breakfast. We can ask her if she has a vacancy."

"But — but —" Skip sputtered, "how will I explain it to Aunt Edwina?"

"Gee, Skip, that's not really my problem. Say I've got a bad back and need a firm mattress. Say I'm allergic to newsprint and can't stand being in the same house with all those old newspapers. Say I need more than two inches of water for a bath." She leaned toward him until their faces were only inches apart. "Say I'm having a nervous breakdown and just might commit murder if I don't get out of that house. I don't give a hoot how you explain it to her, but I'm out of there."

Skip flung himself into an armchair. "Oh, hell, this is really going to piss her off."

"She'll get over it."

He looked troubled. "Last night, after you went to bed, she told me she's left a little something in her will to a few people who've been kind to her in her declining years."

"A little something, huh? That probably means twenty dollars."

"I don't know . . ." He frowned. "Between you and me, she might be getting senile."

"How do you figure that?"

"Well, you saw how thrilled she is with this place," he said, shuddering as he looked around. "Sounded like she practically lives here."

As would Milly if Edwina's home was hers. "It's her life," Milly pointed out as she threw out her arms to take in the big rec room. "And in comparison to her house, it's the Sheraton. You heard her. It's a real swinging place."

"Sarcasm does not become you, Milly."

"So sue me."

Skip sighed. "Milly, if we move out, she might decide to write me out of her will altogether and leave everything to those other people she mentioned."

"And deprive you of that dream house? Heaven forbid."

Ignoring the remark, Skip muttered, "I wish I knew who those people are."

Cutting him a scathing look, she walked over to the television set and switched it on.

Tess was the last person to leave the room after the book discussion. She found Edwina's nephew hovering outside the door. He drew her aside. “Ms. Darcy, could I have a word with you?”

“Of course.” Tess followed him into the rec room. Milly looked up as they entered and reached for the remote control to switch off the TV.

“Do you have any vacancies at your bed and breakfast?” Skip asked.

“Actually, none of the rooms is occupied at the moment. It’s the off-season, and my cook’s on vacation.”

Milly sat forward on the couch. “Would you consider letting us stay with you for a few days?” She glanced toward the hallway, where the members of the book discussion group were heading for the cafeteria. “We can go out for breakfast. We wouldn’t be any trouble at all,” Milly added urgently. “I promise.”

Tess glanced over her shoulder and saw Edwina grab hold of Mercy Bates and say something. Mercy shook off Edwina’s grasp before introducing her to Wally. Edwina took his hand and smiled sweetly while Mercy watched her suspiciously.

Tess turned back to Milly, wondering if Edwina knew her nephew and his wife were planning to lodge elsewhere. “Breakfast would be no problem,” she said, “but my housekeeper is only coming in twice a week this month. You’d have to deal with your own linen, make your own bed.”

“We don’t mind,” Milly said promptly.

Tess hesitated. "Well, all right, I guess. But I thought you were staying with Edwina."

Skip glanced at Milly, who gave him a hard look. "Skip will explain the situation to his aunt," she said.

"To tell you the truth, Ms. Darcy," Skip said, smiling lopsidedly, "we're on our honeymoon. Aunt Edwina's a sweet old thing, but we'd kind of like to have some privacy. I think she'll understand, don't you?"

"Surely," Tess replied, though she wasn't at all sure. But she hadn't realized they were newly wed. Good heavens, the thought of these two young people spending the early days of their marriage at Edwina's made her shudder. Couples should have pleasant memories of their honeymoon. "Then you're welcome at Iris House as long as Edwina's okay with it." She gave them the address, saying they could move in that afternoon. "By the way," she added, "please call me Tess."

Lunch was simple but nourishing — meat loaf, scalloped potatoes, English peas, carrot and raisin salad, and coconut cake for dessert. The first time Tess had eaten at the center, she'd asked Jenny how in the world she managed to provide such good meals for a few dollars a plate. Jenny had said that she didn't. She received money from the federal government to supplement the cost to senior citizens. And since the majority of the people who ate there had low incomes by government standards, she was able to get many staples from a local food bank.

After spending a few days at the center, Tess realized that Jenny and Willis Vercourt were doing a great service for the community and they deserved all the federal money they could get. All in all, Tess had deduced, the Vercourts made a comfortable income. Jenny ran the center, and Willis, a former construction worker, made good use of his carpentry skills by doing necessary repair work around the place. From some of the comments Tess had heard Willis make, being the center's all-around handyman was a full-time job.

In fact, Willis, a swarthy, bulky man of medium height, had worked at unplugging the drain lines in one of the apartments for most of that morning, finishing just before he came in to have lunch.

Once everybody had been served, buffet style, Edwina made a blanket introduction of her nephew and his wife to the group, adding that Skippy was like a son to her. Then she led the two young people to the table where Albert and Anita McBroom sat. Tess noticed Anita's frown, as if she was less than pleased to have Edwina's company. Edwina started talking to Albert, who kept his eyes on his plate. Whatever Edwina was saying, it didn't seem to sit well with Albert, who snatched up his knife and fork as if to fend her off. Instead, he cut himself a bite of meatloaf.

Tess pondered the McBrooms' reactions to Edwina for a moment, but was soon distracted as Willis Vercourt sat down at her table and engaged her in conversation.

"It's mighty good of you to help us out this month, Tess."

"I enjoy it," Tess assured him, "and I can spare the time right now. Next month will be a different story."

"You're doing okay with Iris House, then?"

"So far, so good. I'm booked pretty solid from March to the end of October."

He gave her a weary smile. "You're lucky you were able to completely remodel the house, put in new wiring, get new fixtures and all. You shouldn't have any big repair bills for a long time. Not like this place. Seems like I spend twelve hours a day doing gut work on the center and the apartments. Something's always breaking down."

"Well, they're old buildings."

"Tell me about it. Sometimes I wish we could afford to level the whole place and start over. We're redoing things as we can. This year we plan to competely remodel the kitchen. I hope to have that under way before the health inspector comes back next summer."

"Sounds expensive."

He wobbled one hand in the air. "I can do most of the work myself. New appliances will be costly, but we make a good profit from serving meals, so we'll come up with the money. And Jenny has applied for a government grant. Maybe we'll get a little help there."

"I hope so. It's fortunate that you have the ability to do so much of the work yourself," Tess observed, and Willis agreed, though he confided he'd like to have a little more time off to go fishing.

Across the room, Jenny tapped a knife handle on a tabletop and announced, "Don't forget, everybody. Tomorrow's our monthly potluck, so if you plan to eat with us, bring a covered dish."

After lunch, Tess noticed Skip talking earnestly to Edwina in a corner of the cafeteria. Edwina looked bewildered. Evidently he was telling her that he and Milly would be staying at Iris House for the remainder of their visit. Probably Edwina couldn't fathom why they'd prefer to spend money for a room when they could stay on with her.

But apparently he made her understand, for finally she glanced across the room at Milly, then nodded and patted his arm. It appeared Skip had put the blame for the move on Milly.

As Skip walked away, Tess saw Edwina glance furtively at Mercy Bates and Jenny Vercourt, who were clearing the tables, then, quick as a cat, pluck some packets of sugar from a bowl and stuff them into a pocket of her polyester pants. Edwina made a habit of helping herself to sugar packets, probably other things at the center as well. Jenny had told Tess that she was aware of Edwina's pilfering, having caught her in the act of hiding a roll of toilet tissue under her coat, but had chosen to ignore it. She'd said that if Edwina was too poor to buy sugar and other necessities, she didn't mind letting her take a few things.

Edwina made the rounds of the room, taking sugar packets from bowls. Then, her pants pockets stuffed, she made a beeline for Wally Tanksley, who stood alone just inside the door of the cafeteria, waiting for Mercy. Edwina engaged him in what appeared to be an earnest conversation, emphasizing her words with nods and gestures. Wally said little, but as Edwina talked, he began to look troubled. A couple of times he shook his head, as if denying what Edwina had said, but she merely nodded faster and kept on talking.

Edwina talked to Wally until Mercy came over and put a proprietary hand on his arm. Wally said he had to go and Mercy said she'd walk out to the car with him.

Tess overheard Mercy ask, "What was Edwina saying to you?" as the two left the cafeteria.

"Nothing important," Wally replied.

4

A few minutes later, as Tess left the lunch room and walked down the hall toward the sewing room, where a quilting frame was set up, she saw Edwina reaching into the first locker in the bottom row, the one that Jenny had told her and Ross to keep away from.

"Did you leave something of yours in there?" Tess asked.

Edwina whirled around guiltily, then forced a smile and said, "Oh, no. Albert simply insisted that I take this locker back. He said it's no trouble for him to reach the top row."

Tess had seen Albert grimace in pain when he tried to reach an upper locker. She doubted that Albert would have volunteered to give Edwina the locker, and she wondered how Edwina had persuaded him to do it.

According to Jenny, when Albert and Anita first moved into the center and began taking part in the senior activities, Edwina had befriended Anita. For several weeks, they spent a lot of time together and seemed to be becoming bosom buddies. Then, all of a sudden, something had happened to break up the friendship, and Anita began avoiding the other woman.

Edwina clearly had trouble keeping friends. Tess was tempted to scold her now for being so childish about the lockers. She could easily reach the locker Jenny had given her; reclaiming the disputed locker was a clear case of one-upmanship to taunt Ross with. But Tess kept quiet. It really was none of her business.

She watched Edwina retrieve her sewing basket from the locker and followed her into the sewing room. Tess had paused just inside the room when Albert and Anita McBroom stopped in the hall outside. They were speaking in low tones, obviously unaware that anyone was close enough to hear what they were saying.

"You didn't have to give in to her, Albert," Anita hissed.

"It's simpler that way."

"Simpler?"

"You know what I mean," Albert said. "Whatever Edwina wants, Edwina gets. And don't forget whose fault that is."

"It's so unfair! I hate that woman!"

"Let it go, Anita. It's only a locker."

"It's not the locker! It's the principle of the thing. I am so sick and tired of Edwina's little 'requests.' I can't believe I once thought she was my friend. It makes me so mad the way she keeps hinting about needing repairs on her house when she knows you are no longer able to do physical labor. How long do we have to put up with it?"

"You know the answer to that, too. Till we're dead — or she is." Albert's tone was clipped and hard. "Now, come on. Let's go in."

Albert had joined the quilters several months ago. In addition to a back that tended to go out on him when he put too much strain on it, he suffered from arthritis. His doctor had advised him that exercise might help retard the stiffening of his joints, so in addition to walking a mile each day, he had taken up quilting to give his fingers a workout.

Tess managed to move away from the door before the McBrooms came into view and caught her eavesdropping. She found Joyce Banaker and quickly engaged her in conversation.

"Somehow Edwina has got Albert to give up that locker in the bottom row. She's just put her things back in it."

Joyce shook her head. "The woman is relentless. It's no wonder nobody likes her."

"Mercy makes a valiant effort," Tess said. "She always seems to be defending her."

"Mercy can't stand her."

Surprised, Tess said, "Well, you could have fooled me. I guess it's just Mercy's nature to be kind."

"Maybe, and maybe Mercy is afraid of what Edwina might do to get back at her if she crosses her."

"Perhaps," Tess mused, remembering Mercy's warning that Edwina could be very mean if you got on her wrong side.

"Still," Joyce went on, "I'm always amazed that Mercy keeps coming back for more of Edwina's insults." Her expression turned thoughtful. "There's something between them . . ."

"Between Mercy and Edwina? What do you mean?"

Joyce shook her head. "I'm not sure. But there are hard feelings from way back, I think. Something happened with them a long time ago, maybe as far back as their school days. I asked Mercy about it once, and she said it was all in my imagination. But the way she looked, Tess . . ." Joyce frowned. "So . . . um, tragic, I guess. Oh, well, you know Mercy. She perked up and made a joke out of it."

The two women walked toward the quilting circle. Albert and Anita, along with Opal Bloom, had positioned themselves at the opposite end of the quilting frame from Edwina, who sat between Mercy Bates and Hattie Bloom. As no one seemed to want the chair directly across from Edwina, Tess took it, which put Joyce Banaker on her left.

Because of the seating arrangement, there were often two separate conversations going at the same time, one at each end of the frame.

Tess got out her thimble, needle, and quilting thread and found the place where whoever had sat in her chair the last time had stopped quilting. She made a tiny knot in the end of the thread and pulled it through the quilt top, making sure that the knot nestled between the top and the batting. "I may bring my Log Cabin top down here to get it quilted," she said. "I made it in one of those day-long classes at The Quilter's Nook. I even bought a big lap hoop, thinking I'd quilt it myself, but I never seem to have the time."

"A frame is much better, anyway," Joyce said. "But most people don't have room to leave one set up for weeks or months at a time while they're working on a quilt." She smiled wistfully as she threaded her needle. "Gracious, it seems like my mother had a quilt in a frame in the dining room the whole time I was growing up. We just moved the table and chairs to one side and made do."

"I don't even have a separate dining room in my apartment," Tess said, "nor any other room that's big enough to set up a quilting frame."

Hattie gave her a sly, sidelong look. "You should have plenty of room when you move into Luke's big house."

Tess glanced at her sharply. "Where did you get the idea I'm moving into Luke's house?"

"Oh, I don't know," Hattie said airily. "I must have heard it at the beauty shop when I got my last perm."

"Don't believe everything you hear at the beauty shop. Luke and I haven't decided yet where we'll live."

Joyce looked up from her quilting. "Surely you don't plan to stay in your apartment at Iris House."

"As I said, we haven't decided," Tess told her, but the very thought of moving out of her bed and breakfast stirred up all the anxiety she experienced every time Luke pressed her for a wedding date. It was true that the apartment would be cramped quarters for her and Luke. It was also true that she couldn't bear the thought of moving across town to Luke's house. Everything she had was tied up in her bed and breakfast. She needed to be on hand every morning to greet her guests in the dining room and be available at other times to handle problems as they arose.

Edwina, who had been uncharacteristically silent up till now, suddenly yelped, "Ouch! I stabbed myself."

"That's not exactly news," Joyce muttered without looking at Edwina. "It happens every day."

"Edwina, you refuse to use a thimble," Hattie told her, "so don't complain. And for heaven's sake, don't get blood on the quilt!"

Edwina dabbed at her finger with a tissue. "I learned to quilt without a thimble," she said, "and I just can't get used to one. You can't teach an old dog new tricks."

Mercy suddenly giggled, which caused Edwina to scowl at her. "What's so funny, Mercy?"

"You calling yourself an old dog."

"Is that a dig about my age — which is the same as yours, in case you've forgotten."

"Oh, no. It's just that your remark reminded me of something Gerald once said."

Tess glanced at Mercy and then at Edwina. Mercy rarely mentioned her late husband to the group. For some reason, Gerald's name always seemed to elicit some rude remark from Edwina. Tess had gotten the distinct impression that Edwina was jealous of Mercy's long and apparently happy marriage. She was surprised that Mercy would insert his name into the conversation now, but she thought it had slipped out somehow before Mercy realized what she'd said.

Edwina's back had become as rigid as a two-by-four plank. "Did this remark of dear Gerald's have anything to do with me?"

Mercy's merry smile faded. "I didn't say that."

But Edwina was not mollified. "When it comes to dog tricks, don't get me started on what old Gerald used to say — and do. I don't think you'd want to hear some of it."

Mercy ducked her head, blushing furiously as she fixed her eyes on her quilting. "I didn't mean anything by it, Edwina."

"Of course you did!" Edwina snapped. "You always do when you say things with that simpering smile. Or are you grinning like a Cheshire cat because you've got yourself a new boyfriend?"

Mercy kept her eyes lowered and murmured, "Wally is just a friend, that's all."

"Oh, really?" Edwina went on relentlessly. "You'd never know it, the way you hang onto the man. And by the way, if you insist on wearing that bright-red lipstick, you should learn to put it on straight. I'll bet Wally thought you looked like a clown."

Mercy blushed again and kept her head down, as if waiting for a storm to pass. Tess wanted to tell Edwina to stop picking on sweet, cheerful Mercy. Instead, she said the next thing that came to mind, anything to lighten the tense atmosphere that had descended on the quilters. "Don't you just love the reds and blues in this quilt?"

Joyce picked up on Tess's ploy right away. "Yes, the colors are lovely," she said. "The Williams have a wonderful antique cherry bed with a tall, carved headboard. This will be perfect on it."

At the other end of the frame, a desultory conversation trailed off and Albert caught Joyce's eye and grinned. "Now, how do you know so much about the Reverend Williams's bed, Joyce?"

"I've been in that house many a time, Albert McBroom," Joyce told him, "for the Methodist women's missionary society meetings. And you don't go there even once without Vivian Williams showing you that bed. It belonged to her grandmother, and she's real proud of it. So you can wipe that silly grin off your face."

Albert dipped his head in good-natured acquiescence. When he had first joined the women in the quilting circle, they had been disbelieving, then amused, and finally indulgent, eager to share helpful techniques acquired through years of quilting. Yet none of them had really expected Albert to stick with it long, especially after Ross had called him a seamstress several times and suggested he might start putting lace on his shirt collars. Albert, however, had surprised them and become a fair quilter. Ross Dellin still made a sneering joke now and then about Albert's new hobby, but Albert hadn't let it bother him. Not outwardly, at least. He just steered clear of Ross. But then Albert and Ross had never seemed to Tess to hit it off even before Albert abandoned the domino players in the back room to join the quilters. Like Edwina, Ross had few friends.

"That bed of the Williamses is something to be proud of," Opal said, after a lull in the conversation. "I saw one very similar to it in an auction catalog, priced at thirty-five hundred dollars."

"Imagine that," Anita said. "For a bed."

The conversation turned then to antiques, and everybody seemed to forget the edgy undercurrent created by Edwina's snide innuendo about Mercy's late husband and her ridicule of Mercy's appearance. Everybody except Mercy, that is. Several times, Tess noticed Mercy squinting viciously at Edwina, very unMercy-like behavior. Nor was Edwina unaware of Mercy's perusal, for once she looked to one side quickly enough to make eye contact with Mercy, and her mouth curled slowly in cunning amusement, as if she knew something scandalous about the other woman — or the late Gerald — and might broadcast it if provoked. She probably didn't know anything truly shocking, but maybe Mercy wasn't sure of that.

The quilting circle broke up two hours later, some of the seniors going home immediately, others moving to the game room behind the cafeteria to play dominoes.

Before leaving, Tess walked around the room, picking discarded pieces of quilting thread from the carpet. Anita McBroom had stopped to rearrange her quilting supplies, and as Tess carried the threads she'd gathered to the wastebasket, Edwina, the only other person left in the room, paused beside Anita, whose head was bent over her open sewing basket.

"It was so sweet of Albert to give me back my locker, Anita," Edwina said, her tone snide rather than grateful.

Anita's head shot up. Her eyes blazed. "Jenny will make you give it up again as soon as I tell her that you badgered Albert into it."

Edwina stared at her, smirking. "I don't think you want to do that, Anita," she said.

Anita watched Edwina march from the room. Her hands were shaking.

Tess walked over to her. "Are you all right, Anita?"

Anita jumped and clutched her basket to her breast, startled by Tess's voice. Evidently Anita hadn't known Tess was still in the room.

"I'm fine," Anita said curtly.

"I'll tell Jenny that Edwina's taken the locker back from Albert," Tess said.

"No!" Anita gripped Tess's arm. "Don't do that, Tess. Edwina will think I put you up to it."

"Anita, I've seen how painful it is for Albert to reach those lockers in the top rows. Edwina shouldn't be allowed to get away with this."

"Let it go, Tess. It's not worth the trouble Edwina would cause. Trust me."

"What can she do but whine and complain?"

"Oh, she'll think of something much worse than that. You don't know Edwina like I do. She has a devious mind."

Which seemed to be the opinion of everybody who knew Edwina very well.

"For heaven's sake, Anita. When you give in to her like this, you only encourage her to keep taking advantage of you."

"Don't worry about it, Tess."

"How did she get Albert to agree to switch lockers in the first place?"

"Albert would rather give in than fuss about it. I — I have to go, Tess. I have some laundry to do. Just don't say anything to Jenny, okay?"

"Well . . . all right," Tess agreed. "But if you change your mind . . ."

Anita shook her head and walked away, her lips pursed tightly, repressing something. Tess wondered what.

Anita hurried back to the small efficiency apartment where she and Albert would live out their last years, the years she had once looked forward to, the years that were supposed to be golden but that in their case had turned out to be a cheap imitation. She closed the door behind her and immediately experienced the sensation of the walls crowding in on her from all sides. Her heart pounded too fast.

She'd suffered several anxiety attacks in the last year and by now she knew the signs. She'd learned how to deal with them. She lay down on the couch, closed her eyes, tried to make her mind a blank, and practiced taking in deep, slow breaths of air. Within a few minutes, her heartbeat had slowed, and when she opened her eyes, the walls were back where they belonged.

But still far too close together, she thought as her glance slid over the tiny kitchen at one end of the living room, then to the door at the other end, which led to a bedroom and a tiny bathroom with a narrow stall shower and no tub. Anita still missed the long, luxurious bubble baths that had always helped her to relax at the end of the day. She'd had a small tape player in her bathroom back in Texas, and she'd played Mozart or Beethoven while she lazed in the warm water. Thinking too much about the lovely three-bedroom home they'd had to sell before moving to Victoria Springs brought on dark depressions, but sometimes she couldn't stop herself.

While she and Albert were working — he as a high school principal, she as a secretary in the school superintendent's office — she had never imagined herself spending her final years in such meager, cramped quarters. But that was before they knew that Albert would have to take early retirement and they would have to move.

Anita's gaze blurred as her eyes filled with tears. It wasn't fair. They'd both tried to live upright lives. Childless themselves, they'd chosen jobs where they felt they could help guide young people in the right direction, and they'd worked hard. But they'd enjoyed their hobbies, too — gardening and hiking — before Albert's arthritis had got so bad. And the gourmet dinner club they'd belonged to had been great fun. One summer, they'd even gone to San Francisco for cooking classes with a well-known chef. They had loved the challenge of trying to outdo the other couples in their dinner club in preparing unique and exotic meals. It had been a good life, one that she had expected to continue after retirement.

They, who had never purposely harmed anyone in their lives, weren't supposed to end up like this.

She knew that dwelling on the past did her no good, but today she couldn't push it aside. The injustice done to them was like a pain that would not go away for which there was no treatment. It eased a little when she could occupy her mind with something else, but still it was there, waiting to surface again at the first opportunity.

Anita wished she could take Albert's advice and learn to be content. *If you can't get what you want, then want what you get,* he'd say, repeating a maxim he learned from his mother. And perhaps she could have learned if Edwina Riley hadn't entered their lives. Hardly a day passed when Anita didn't regret that they'd chosen to settle in their low-income apartment behind the senior citizens center, where meeting Edwina had been inevitable. But they were stuck now; they could not afford to move again.

At night, when she couldn't sleep, she entertained herself by constructing scenarios in which Edwina met a terrible end. An accident in which Edwina was thrown from a bus or a train to writhe in pain for hours before she died. Or a long and painful illness that ended in Edwina's dying alone and friendless in her squalid house. Or a car accident that left the driver unharmed but Edwina paralyzed from the neck down, lying in a nursing home at the mercy of low-paid health aides, never having any visitors, no longer able to form words and spill out the vitriol that poisoned anybody who got too close to her. Anita pictured herself paying a single, final visit to the paralyzed Edwina to tell her what a despicable person she was.

Sometimes, like today, Anita thought she could actually kill the woman herself, if there was a chance in the world she could get away with it. Once she had even found herself looking up books on poison in the library's card catalogue.

She heard Albert at the door and sat up, quickly smoothed her hair into place, and straightened her dress.

When he opened the door, she had fixed a smile on her face.

5

When Tess returned to Iris House, Milly was waiting in a red Honda Civic at the curb. She got out of the car, carrying a small suitcase, and joined Tess on the sidewalk. "Skip's staying at his aunt's house for a while," Milly said. "I'll pick him up later."

Tess unlocked the front door. "Come on in, and we'll get you settled." Milly followed her up the broad staircase to the first room on the right at the top of the stairs.

"Annabel Jane Room," Milly said, reading the brass plate on the door as Tess unlocked it. "That's an odd name for a room. Who's Annabel Jane?"

Tess pushed open the door for Milly to enter, then followed her in.

"Not who. What," Tess said. "Annabel Jane is the name of a well-known iris, well-known to iris growers, anyway. All the guest rooms are named for irises."

"Oh, I get it," Milly said. "This is Iris House. I saw your sign in the yard." She set her suitcase beside the bed and slowly turned around, taking in the delicately scrolled white-and-brass bed with its puffy white coverlet and lacy dust ruffle and throw pillows, the white wicker baskets overflowing with ivy, the chaise longue upholstered in lavender and spring-green floral chintz.

Milly sighed happily and a smile erased the strain from her face. "This is fabulous. I would never have imagined there was anything this classy in Victoria Springs. Thank you for letting Skip and me move in."

Milly's condescension to Tess's town was almost mitigated by her thanks, but not quite. "You're welcome," Tess told her. She pointed at the wicker dresser. "Your keys are in the top right-hand dresser drawer. One opens the door to this room, the other is for the main door downstairs." Tess checked the furniture for dust, but Nedra had been there the day before and everything was spotlessly clean. "The linen closet is at the end of the hall on the left. Help yourself to whatever you need. On the right, across from the linen closet, you'll see a spiral staircase. That leads to the library in the tower. You're welcome to go up there whenever you want to read or to bring books down to your room."

Milly sank onto the chaise. "I've died and gone to heaven. I'm going to love it here."

"Good." Tess went to the door. "I can serve breakfast in the dining room downstairs any time between seven and eight-thirty. Since you and Skip are my only guests, you get to choose."

"Eight, then."

"All right. My apartment's downstairs, too — the door on your left as you enter. My phone number's in the booklet by the phone if you need anything else."

"I'm sure I'll be fine. Thanks again."

Milly shrugged off her coat, settled happily into the chaise, and closed her eyes as Tess left, quietly shutting the door behind her.

Visiting an elderly aunt seemed an odd way to spend a honeymoon, Tess mused as she descended the stairs. Obviously it was important to Skip to be here, and equally obvious that Milly wasn't happy about it. Now that the young couple were at Iris House, perhaps they could begin to enjoy their stay, in spite of Milly's seeming disdain for Victoria Springs — that is, unless Skip planned to spend all his days with Edwina, leaving his new wife to fend for herself.

Lying on the chaise, Milly felt her clenched muscles start to relax. By the time Edwina had agreed to leave the center and Milly had driven her and Skip to Edwina's house — Skip sat in the back that trip — her nerves had been pinging like taut strings being plucked by a fiddler at a country hoedown. Edwina had decided to sit like a stump in the car, talking, until Milly had the steering wheel in a two-handed death grip to keep from screaming at the old woman to shut up and get out. Finally Skip had evidently realized how close to a blowup she was and had pushed Milly's seat forward, her chest squashed against the steering wheel, to squeeze out of the car and open Edwina's door. "We better get you inside out of the cold, Auntie."

Once Edwina and Skip were out of the car, Milly had burned rubber getting away, smiling grimly as she imagined Skip trying to excuse her haste. By the time Tess Darcy returned to Iris House, Milly was on the verge of leaving altogether, speeding out of Victoria Springs and back to Fort Worth without Skip.

Then Tess drove up, and she'd decided to at least take a look at a room, which was so much lovelier than she had expected that she'd immediately wanted to move in, lock the door, and sleep for a week. Once she'd caught up on her sleep, she'd check out the library in the tower.

She was so put out with Skip that she almost wished he'd decided to spend his nights at Edwina's. But, as he kept pointing out, for a man who was supposed to be on his honeymoon, that would look too odd. He'd told Milly to come back for him at six-thirty and they'd go somewhere for dinner before returning to Iris House — on her credit card, of course. Meantime, he hoped to wheedle information about her estate, as he called it, from Edwina. He was going to tell her the lie about naming his first daughter after her and hint that she should give second thoughts to leaving other people "a little something." Somehow he would manage to suggest that he could use that money to start an educational fund for his future daughter, Edwina's future grandniece and namesake. There had been an uncommon urgency about Skip as he told Milly this latest plan, adding that he was convinced Edwina couldn't live much longer. She'd gone downhill alarmingly, he said, since he'd last seen her.

The whole thing was getting so tangled up with Skip's lies and schemes that Milly wanted no further part of it. After the potluck luncheon at the center tomorrow, she would avoid Edwina for the rest of their stay. At lunch Edwina had extracted Skip's promise that he and Milly would be there tomorrow. After that, Milly had told Skip, he could say she wasn't feeling well. He'd managed to twist that to his advantage, too, saying he could use it to suggest to his aunt that Milly's symptoms were a lot like morning sickness. Wouldn't it be wonderful, he'd say, if Milly was already pregnant with little Edwina?

Just before Milly drifted into sleep, she told herself that she no longer cared what Skip told his aunt. She just wanted out of it.

Having stopped at the grocery store and pharmacy on the way home, Joyce Banaker didn't turn into her own street until after five o'clock. Dusk was settling over the block of small frame houses and venerable old trees, their bare branches spreading upward like gnarled black fingers reaching for the gray sky.

Eager to learn how much the workmen had accomplished on the garage foundation that day, Joyce was already turning into her driveway before she realized that something was wrong.

She got out of her car and stared at the street in front of her house. All at once, her heart skidded against her breastbone. Her late husband's beloved Mustang was gone. She laid a gloved hand over her chest where her heart was hammering.

Don't panic, she told herself.

The workmen had probably moved it. She had understood that the foundation work might take several days, but perhaps they had finished sooner than expected and had moved the Mustang back into the garage as a favor to her. But even as these thoughts skittered through her head, she remembered that she had left the car locked and had taken the key with her.

As she circled around a corner of the house and headed for the backyard, she saw that the garage door was still up, as it had been that morning. There was evidence that the workmen had been there, but they were gone now. As dark as it was inside the garage, she could still see, half-way there, that the Mustang wasn't shrouded in the shadowy interior.

Knowing it was futile, she walked all the way around the garage and then the house. The car had disappeared. Digging her keys out of her coat pocket, Joyce hurried to the front door and unlocked it. She found the business card the head workman had given her and dialed the number.

"Mr. Jason, this is Joyce Banaker. You worked on my garage today."

"Yes, ma'am. We determined the extent of your problem, which is pretty bad, but we can fix it. We'll —"

"Never mind that now. Did you happen to notice a blue '65 Mustang parked in front of my house."

"Yes, I did. That's a dilly of a car, Mrs. Banaker. If you ever want to sell it —"

Joyce cut in, nearly frantic now. "It's gone."

He hesitated briefly. "Why, yes, ma'am. The wrecker came and got it this afternoon."

"What wrecker?"

"Well . . . er . . . it was just a wrecker, Mrs. Banaker. I assumed you were having it worked on."

"I didn't call any wrecker!"

"Oh, gee, I'm sorry, Mrs. Banaker. I didn't know that. If I had, I'd have tried to stop them."

"Did you see a sign on that wrecker, something to identify it?"

He thought a minute. "There may have been

some lettering, but to tell you the truth, I wasn't paying that much attention. The guy acted like he had a right to be there," he added apologetically. "Let me think, now. The truck cab was dark green. I remember that. You might call the city transportation garage. They've got a wrecker and probably know who else in town does."

"Thank you, Mr. Jason." Unsteadily Joyce placed the receiver in the cradle. Fumbling awkwardly with the directory, because her hands were trembling, she finally managed to find the number of the city's transportation garage.

While Joyce struggled to keep from bursting into tears, she explained her dilemma to the man who answered. "Our wrecker's dark green, all right," he said. "The day shift guys have already left. I just got here. Let me go look around on the lot." After what seemed an endless time, he came back. "We got a Mustang like the one you described here, ma'am. I checked the log we keep. Looks like we got a complaint this morning that it had been abandoned in your neighborhood. We pick up abandoned cars and sell them at auction a couple of times a year."

"That car was not abandoned!" Joyce cried, her control beginning to slip. "It was parked on the street while my garage is being repaired."

"Well, I'm sorry, ma'am, but we did get a complaint —"

"I don't care how many complaints you got!

That's my car, and I want it brought back right now!"

"The wrecker driver's gone for the day. We couldn't bring it back till tomorrow at the earliest."

"I'll just walk down there and drive it back then. You're not far from my house."

"I'm sorry, ma'am, but I can't let anything leave the lot without my supervisor's okay. He'll be here tomorrow."

"Then I'll come down in the morning and drive it back. What time should I be there?" Joyce demanded.

"Depends."

"On what?"

"We have to see your title before we can let it go. And you'll have to pay the ninety-dollar towing charge."

"I don't believe this!" Joyce shrieked, finally losing her composure altogether. "The city stole that car from in front of my house and I have to pay for the towing?"

"Now, just a minute, Mrs. Banaker. Nobody stole nothing. We got a complaint, and we followed up on it. That's our job."

"Didn't it occur to anybody to check with me first?"

"They usually do check with whoever lives closest to the abandoned car."

"It wasn't abandoned," Joyce yelled at him.

"Right. Anyway, you must've been gone when they came."

"They should have waited till I got back before driving off with my Mustang. I'm —" Joyce clamped her lips together to keep from saying anything further. She'd just end up crying in frustration, and it wasn't this man's fault. He wasn't even on duty when they took the car away. "I'll be down there in the morning. And there'd better not be a scratch on that car or I'll take the city to court." She banged the receiver down without waiting for his response.

She walked into the kitchen and gripped the edge of the counter, willing herself to calm down. She was so angry that her whole body shook and she thought that the top of her head might fly off. After a few moments, she believed she had gained enough control to confront the person who was responsible for her car being hauled downtown.

Oh, she had no doubt who was behind the disappearance of the Mustang. She knew of only one person who was cruel enough to pull a stunt like this.

Never having removed her coat, she marched out her front door and across the yard to Edwina's porch and up to the door, where she banged loudly. She waited and knocked again, then kicked the wall of the house for good measure. She'd seen a light in the kitchen when she crossed the yard. Edwina never left a light on in the house when she was gone. In fact, she walked around in the dark half the time when she was there, trying to save a few pennies on electricity. Joyce knocked a third time and yelled, "Edwina, I know you're in there!"

But nobody came to the door. Joyce hesitated. It was an effort not to try kicking the door in, but she'd probably only break a toe.

The sneaky bitch was hiding from her. Joyce had no doubt about it as she turned and stomped down the steps and crossed to her own house. Edwina couldn't hide forever.

Joyce had tolerated Edwina's vicious tricks for weeks now, but reporting the Mustang as an abandoned car was more than she was prepared to put up with. Edwina was going to pay for this.

6

Mercy Bates took special care with her makeup that evening before leaving for choir practice at church. Edwina's catty remark about her lipstick had hurt her deeply, even though she should be used to Edwina's spitefulness by now. And this afternoon she'd almost asked for it by mentioning Gerald, which she tried never to do in Edwina's hearing. Today she'd been so pleased that Wally had come for the book discussion that she'd let down her guard and Gerald's name had slipped out, and Edwina had reacted predictably.

Mercy reminded herself that Gerald had loved her, not Edwina, never Edwina. Once Mercy had gotten over what she had thought of as Gerald's betrayal — what she later came to realize was Edwina's betrayal — she and Gerald had had a long and happy marriage. Most of the time she could pity Edwina instead of hating her. Not today, though. She sighed and patted her curly black hair into place, determined not to let Edwina spoil what was left of the day.

She chose a soft, pink shade for her lips, applied it, and stepped back a little to survey her handiwork in the bathroom mirror. She hated to admit that Edwina was right, but perhaps pink was more flattering than red. She gave her nose a final pat with the powder puff and smiled at the thought of perhaps seeing Wally at church. When she'd gone out to the car with him at the center, she'd reminded him of choir practice, but he'd seemed undecided about whether he would be there. In fact, he'd seemed evasive and in an unusual hurry to leave the center. Was she being too clingy, taking too much for granted? She must watch that. Gerald would always be the love of her life, but Gerald was gone, and she liked Wally a lot, even though he had been divorced so long that he was probably set in his bachelor ways. Maybe he liked his life just as it was. As for Mercy, she enjoyed a man's company and would love to be married again. It got so lonely, living by herself. But it was too soon to let Wally know that the thought of marriage had ever entered her head. She didn't want to scare him away.

She tapped a polished fingernail against the reflection of her face in the mirror. "Friendship, Mercy, that's all you're looking for," she told herself. At least, that's what she must convey to Wally.

When she entered the church a few minutes later, about a dozen choir members were already there. She saw Wally right away. He was talking to the Stanleys, a youngish couple who were choir mainstays.

Mercy spoke to several people, waiting until the Stanleys moved off, before she made her way to Wally's side.

"I see you made it," she said.

"Yeah," said the usually articulate Wally.

"The book discussion group enjoyed having you today. We could use a few more people with some new opinions to offer."

"I probably won't be able to come on a regular basis."

Mercy kept smiling determinedly. "Oh, that's all right. Just come when you can. By the way, I wanted to invite you to the covered-dish luncheon tomorrow at the center. We have some wonderful cooks, and there's always more good food than we can eat."

He didn't seem to want to meet her gaze. "Er . . . I wouldn't want you to count on me. I need to work on my car."

"Surely you could come for an hour. You have to eat lunch anyway. I could get somebody to pick you up."

"No, thanks, Mercy. Oh, there's Jack Long. I need to have a word with him. Excuse me."

Mercy felt her face crumple as she watched him hurry away. Never had she seen such an abrupt about-face in a person's behavior. Lately, he'd sought her out at choir practice, sat beside her at church. Once, when they bumped into each other in town, he'd even bought her a sandwich. Now, he was obviously trying to avoid her.

She thought back over the afternoon. He'd come to the center at her invitation, joined her for the book discussion and lunch. He'd acted the same as always, talking and laughing, as though he really enjoyed being there. But after lunch, she'd noticed he'd distanced himself, and he'd been in a big hurry to leave the center. What had caused the change?

Or who?

Suddenly she remembered the way Edwina had held Wally's hand too long and smiled ever so sweetly when she introduced them. And how Edwina had sought him out to talk while she helped clear the tables. Edwina must have told him something that made him change his mind about her — Edwina's way of retaliating for her verbal slip about Gerald when they were quilting. There was no other explanation for Wally's behavior just now.

Suddenly tears of rage pricked Mercy's eyes. Every really bad thing that had happened to her in her life had been Edwina's fault. The woman was like a rabid animal that had sunk its teeth into Mercy's throat and wouldn't let go until she drew her last breath. For the first time in years, Mercy was so furious with Edwina that she wished her dead.

Head down, she hurried from the sanctuary and went into the ladies' restroom, where she locked herself in a stall until she could regain her composure. She dabbed at her eyes with a tissue, careful not to smear her mascara.

Not again, she vowed. She would not allow Edwina to destroy her chance for happiness again. Maybe if she explained to Wally that Edwina was a liar who enjoyed hurting people, he'd believe her, but she didn't want to face him until she knew what Edwina had said about her. Knowing Edwina, Mercy thought it could be almost anything.

Tomorrow she would force Edwina to tell her.

Oh, sure. When had she ever forced Edwina to do anything?

She had another idea. She'd call Tess Darcy and ask her to find out what Edwina had said to Wally. Edwina seemed to like Tess and she never tried to browbeat her as she did so many other people. If anybody could find out what Edwina had done to sour her friendship with Wally, Mercy thought, it would be Tess.

Luke waved a hand in front of Tess's face to get her attention and said once again, "Sweetheart, it's not your problem."

After going out for dinner, they'd returned to Iris House to watch the late evening news. They'd barely removed their coats when Mercy Bates called. Mercy's voice had been thick with tears as she blurted, "Please, Tess, you have to help me." Then she had explained how Wally had treated her at church that evening and her belief that Edwina was the cause. She told Tess what she wanted her to do. Now Tess was so angry with Edwina that she had been able to think of little else since. The woman went around throwing off bad vibes like a skunk spraying his stink on everything in sight.

Tess reached for Primrose, her gray Persian, who'd curled up between them, and moved her to one side so that she could scoot closer to Luke. Primrose growled to make known her displeasure at having her nap interrupted, then closed her eyes and went back to sleep.

Tess took Luke's hand and sighing, laid her head on his shoulder. "It's just that Edwina terrorizes people."

Luke laughed. "She's a little old lady, sweetheart."

"In this case, her disposition has gotten worse with age. And Mercy is the perfect victim. She doesn't want trouble with anybody. So she lets Edwina walk all over her."

"That's right. She lets her. It's Mercy's problem, and I doubt at her age that she's going to reinvent herself."

"You're probably right."

He kissed her brow. "Accept what you can't change, love, and don't let it get to you."

Tess was torn between appreciation of a fiancé who was trying to distract her from troubling thoughts and outrage at Edwina Riley.

"Thank you for being such a steadying influence, Luke." Her hand squeezing his told him that she appreciated more than his words about her current dilemma.

Luke grinned and put his arm around her, drawing her down with him as he sprawled on the couch, his head on its upholstered arm. Having been scooted farther down the couch, Primrose yowled as if she'd been struck, then rose, stretched, flipped her tail, jumped off the couch, and padded down the hall toward Tess's bedroom and her own soft pillow-bed.

"Good night, Primrose," Tess called after her.

The cat did not even look around.

"We pushed her out," Tess murmured.

"Good. There isn't room for the three of us on this couch." He nuzzled Tess's hair, telling her that he had more in mind this evening than watching the television news.

Tess did, too, but right now she had to think about how to approach Edwina on Mercy's behalf.

"Luke, did you know that Edwina and Mercy were high school classmates?"

Wrapping both arms around her, he settled more comfortably into the couch. "Nope, but then I barely know those women."

"Joyce Banaker thinks Mercy and Edwina still have hard feelings from something that happened back then. Whatever it was, it must be something Edwina can hold over Mercy's head, because Mercy is always trying to placate her."

"Maybe Mercy is just a forgiving soul. What's the point in harboring hard feelings for fifty years?"

"Mmm," Tess murmured, "I'd agree except for what Mercy said on the telephone a while ago. I asked her why Edwina had it in for her and, Luke, she broke down and started to cry. Then she told me that Edwina had been the bane of her existence for as long as she could remember and that she was sick and tired of it and she wasn't going to let Edwina hurt her any more. She said she was going to put a stop to it once and for all."

"She's too afraid of the woman even to confront her," Luke said. "How does she propose to keep Edwina from doing whatever she sets out to do?"

"She didn't say. Frankly, I think she was so upset she hardly realized what she was saying. If Edwina would cooperate, I think Mercy would still be willing to let bygones be bygones."

"Sensible woman," Luke mused, "but not much backbone, from what you say."

"I know, and today Mercy's new gentleman friend came to the center and Edwina took him aside for a talk. Mercy saw him at choir practice later and said he was very unfriendly. She's sure Edwina told him something awful about her and asked me to try to find out what."

"Tess," he said again gently, "it isn't your problem. You should tell Mercy to fight her own battles."

"I just don't think she can."

He heaved a sigh. "I can see I'm wasting my breath."

She twisted sideways so that her body was tucked into the narrow space between Luke and the back of the couch. "I'm sorry for spoiling your evening. I'll shut up and let you listen to the news."

"It sounds like the same stuff they broadcast at six." He stretched out his arm for the remote control and turned off the set.

"Let's talk about something else then," Tess said.

He found her mouth and they settled into a lingering kiss. Finally Luke murmured, "Excellent idea, love. Let's talk about the wedding. Have you decided on a date?"

"No — not exactly."

"Can we agree on a month, at least?"

"Oh, Luke, I want to, but first we have to decide where we'll live. I simply can't bear the thought of leaving Iris House."

He kissed her again. "Then we'll live here. Problem solved. Now, about the wedding date . . ."

"But there isn't enough room here. And what about your office?"

"I'll keep my office in my house. Sidney would be thrilled to move into my living quarters there and keep an eye on things."

"You'd actually move out?"

"For you, my love, yes, I would."

Tess combed her fingers through his blond hair, lifting it off his forehead. "We'd be terribly cramped here. Oh, Luke, do you really think we could manage?"

"I've been giving that a lot of thought, and I believe I know how we can manage quite well."

"Really? How?"

He placed a finger over her lips. "I'll tell you about it when I have it all worked out."

"When will that be?"

"Soon. For now, how does an April wedding strike you?"

She smiled and brushed kisses across his forehead and down his cheek. He was so dear. "Aunt Dahlia insists that we have a formal wedding. She wants to help me plan how the church will be decorated and organize a reception at the country club."

"Ah, mustn't disappoint Aunt Dahlia. And she is an organizer, I have to admit."

"I would hate to disappoint her, Luke. She does love planning celebrations, and since Cinny doesn't seem to have a wedding on the horizon, I'm the next best thing."

"I don't know about Cinny. Cody Yount seems to have become a permanent fixture in her life."

"I don't think they've talked about marriage. Not yet, anyway. But about our wedding — I'll want my family here, of course. Dad will need plenty of notice in order to get away. I don't think we could pull it all together by April.

How about June?"

"June," he said, fingering the top button of her blouse, "will be perfect."

Tess had been asleep a couple of hours when a noise awakened her. She sat up in her bed in the dark, cocking her head to pick up another sound. Nothing. She lay back down, wondering if she'd actually heard something or only dreamed it. At any rate, she'd worry about it if she didn't look around.

She turned on the bedside lamp, grabbed her robe, putting it on as she slid her feet into the satin scuffs beside her bed. Primrose, on her pillow in the corner of the bedroom, yawned and stretched, but went back to sleep.

Tess walked through the apartment, turning on lights. Quietly she opened the door into the foyer and peered out. She always left the foyer light on, and it illuminated what she could see of the guest parlor. Everything appeared undisturbed.

Leaving her apartment door open, she crossed the foyer to the guest parlor, from where she could see that the kitchen light was on. Tess was sure she hadn't left it that way. She walked through the parlor and guest dining room and paused in the kitchen doorway.

Skip Hector sat at the kitchen table, his head in his hands. An empty glass sat beside him.

"Skip?"

His head jerked up. "Whoa, Tess. You scared

me. I didn't know another soul was awake."

"I thought I heard something, came out to check."

"I guess it was me, running water for a drink." He smiled apologetically. "I'm sorry, Tess. I couldn't sleep and came down here to keep from disturbing Milly. I tried to be quiet. I hope it's okay just to sit here for a while."

"It's fine, Skip." Tess hesitated, wanting to ask why he couldn't sleep. Was he worried about something? But it wasn't her place to intrude on a guest's privacy. "Just turn the light off when you go back up, please."

"I will."

She left him there and went back to bed.

7

Tess was in the kitchen the next morning at eight, when Skip and Milly came downstairs. "Good morning," she called to them. "There's coffee and juice on the buffet. Help yourselves."

She'd already defrosted a ham and egg casserole and as Milly and Skip settled at the dining table with coffee, she popped the casserole into the microwave. Then she removed a pan of Gertie's light-as-air croissants from the warming oven. Butter, honey and several kinds of jelly and jam were already on the table, along with a platter of sliced honeydew melon and cantaloupe.

In the dining room, Skip said, "We have to pick up Aunt Edwina and take her to the senior citizens center."

"You pick her up," Milly said curtly. "I'll stay here and read till you get back. We'll find some place nice for lunch."

"Today's the potluck at the center. Aunt Edwina's expecting us to eat with her. We promised, remember."

Tess had removed the casserole from the

oven and had been about to carry it to the dining room, but Milly's groan made her hesitate. She didn't want to interrupt the newlyweds in what sounded like a disagreement in the making.

"You promised, Skip. And I'm up to here with trying to please dear old Edwina."

"Be patient a little longer," Skip said in a wheedling tone. "We'll have lunch out tomorrow."

"What makes you think I'll still be here tomorrow?" Milly muttered.

"Aw, honey, don't be that way." There was a long pause. Then Skip added in a falsely bright tone, "I'm making real headway with Aunt Edwina. I told you how thrilled she was when I said we'd talked it over and wanted to name our first daughter for her."

"You're making headway? What does that mean, Skip?"

"I told her we wanted to start an education fund for our daughter right away. She said she thought that was a fine idea."

"So? I'm sure she didn't offer to make the first deposit. Skip, what's the point? How many more boring days am I supposed to spend here while you talk your aunt into leaving every niggling little dime she's squirreled away in a sock somewhere to you — and our nonexistent daughter. We're probably talking about a few hundred dollars here, tops. I'm telling you I can't take this much longer. I'm ready to go back to Fort Worth and leave you to hitch your way home. I'm sick and tired of the whole business."

"I know, sweetheart. I'm not exactly having a blast here, either, but I'm willing to put up with the old bat for the sake of our future. Just a few more days, I promise."

The couple were so intent on their conversation that the possibility they could be overheard from the kitchen had evidently not occurred to them. To remind them of her presence, Tess cleared her throat loudly and rattled the foil as she removed it from the croissants.

When she reached the dining room with the casserole and bread, Milly was staring glumly out the dining room window and Skip stood at the buffet, topping off his coffee. There were dark smudges around his eyes, evidence of a sleepless night. Tess wondered how long he'd sat in the kitchen after she'd gone back to bed.

Later that morning, Tess set her still-warm potato casserole — one of Gertie's recipes — on the table at the senior citizens center with the rest of the covered dishes, all of which were labeled with the owners' names. Peeking under a few foil covers, she saw that Anita had brought a delicious-looking broccoli and raisin salad and Mercy a casserole whose main ingredient appeared to be squash. There was Don Bob's chicken salad, and a basket of fat, fluffy dinner rolls, Hattie's contribution. Opal had made a ham casserole. Somebody, probably Ross, had brought a plate of the local bakery's famous chocolate cream cheese bars.

Predictably, Edwina had contributed her usual bowl of macaroni and cheese made from a box mix. Joyce said she got them at the supermarket, five for a dollar, and the cheese wasn't real. Peering a little closer, Tess saw that Edwina had added a creative touch this time. Looked like chunks of Spam. *Ugh,* she thought, as she hastily recovered the bowl.

Joyce came in and set a vegetable relish plate with onion dip on the table. "Have you seen Edwina?" she asked.

"No, but her macaroni and cheese is here, so she's around somewhere. Probably in the sewing room." Today they were having the quilting circle before lunch.

Without another word, Joyce turned around and left the dining room, walking fast and with determination. A few moments later, Joyce said in a loud voice, "Edwina, come out in the hall. I want to talk to you."

Wonder what Edwina's done now? Tess thought. She could see the hallway from where she stood. Edwina strolled out of the sewing room, a look of puzzled innocence on her face.

"What're you screeching about, Joyce?"

"I'm sending you a bill for ninety dollars," Joyce said, "to pay for the tow truck that hauled my Mustang."

"I don't know what you're talking about," Edwina said.

"You do, too, dammit!" Which told Tess how very upset Joyce was. Joyce never swore.

Edwina planted her hands on her hips and sniffed. "No, I don't."

"Then let me refresh your memory," Joyce said evenly, reaching out and snatching Edwina's arm. "You called the city and reported that the Mustang had been abandoned in front of my house — after I'd made a point of telling you it would be parked there for a few days. I've tolerated the trash department leaving me reminders because of your complaints, but this is too much. They hauled off the Mustang yesterday. I had to go down to the city garage and claim it. I had to pay them ninety dollars before they'd let me have it."

"I'm sorry about your stupid old Mustang, but you have no proof I was the one who called them!"

"Don't bother denying it, Edwina. They told me it was a woman. Besides, who else would play such a dirty trick on a neighbor?"

"Dirty trick? If you want to talk about dirty tricks, what about getting up a petition to try to force me to spend money I don't have to fix up my house?"

"Don't change the subject. I'm sending you the bill, Edwina."

"You know I don't have ninety dollars! I'm not paying you a dime! Now, leave me alone."

Edwina wrenched her arm from Joyce's grasp and walked away.

"You'll pay," Joyce yelled after her, "or I'll take you to small claims court!"

"Be my guest!" Edwina yelled back. "It'll be my word against yours. Anyway, you can't get blood out of a turnip."

Tess walked into the hall, where Joyce was gripping the frame of the sewing room door with both hands, her face drained of color.

"I couldn't help overhearing, Joyce," Tess said.

"I'm sure everyone heard," Joyce replied, "and I don't care." She dropped her hands and squared her shoulders. "Edwina won't get away with this. She's going to pay me that ninety dollars, or I'll make her wish she had."

"Joyce, are you sure it's worth the hassle?" Tess could hardly believe she was using the same argument that Anita had used with her yesterday, an argument she had debated at the time. But the more she learned about Edwina, the better she could see Anita's point.

"It's worth it," Joyce replied grimly, as she released the doorframe and straightened her shoulders. "I'm tired of being harassed. It's finished. I'll see to that, whatever it takes." Her jaw set stubbornly, she marched into the sewing room.

Skip and Milly Hector came out to the hall from the rec room. "What's going on?" Skip asked.

"Your aunt and Joyce Banaker are having a disagreement," Tess said. "I gather somebody reported Joyce's Mustang as an abandoned car and the city towed it away."

"And she thinks Aunt Edwina did it?" Skip asked.

"Did she?" Tess asked.

Skip looked bewildered. "Why would she do that?" He glanced at Milly, who lifted her shoulders as though to say, don't ask me, but her expression said that she thought Edwina quite capable of such a thing.

"Let's go to town and look around until lunchtime," Milly said, tugging on Skip's sleeve.

"Okay. Tess, will you tell Aunt Edwina we'll be back to have lunch with her?"

"Sure," Tess agreed, and tried to think how to get Edwina alone so that she could question her about Wally Tanksley. In spite of Luke's advice to stay out of it, she wanted to help Mercy undo whatever trouble Edwina had made between Mercy and Wally.

The quilters, who'd all heard the confrontation between Joyce and Edwina, were subdued as they worked. Occasionally someone would glance at Joyce to see if she was going to keep after Edwina, but Joyce ignored the other woman for the full hour. Even Edwina, except for yelping when she stabbed her fingers with her needle, which she seemed to do even more often than usual today, was uncharacteristically quiet. And poor Mercy kept her head down, repeatedly dabbing at her eyes and nose with a tissue. Finally, near the end of the session, Edwina apparently couldn't keep quiet any longer and flared, "For God's sake, stop that sniffing and snorting, Mercy!"

At that, Mercy got up abruptly and left the room, sobbing.

Later, Tess noticed as the quilting circle broke up that Edwina was lingering behind the others, rearranging the supplies in her sewing basket and no doubt trying to avoid Joyce. With a half hour before lunch time, Tess saw her chance to talk to Edwina alone.

"I'm going to have to get some new quilting needles," Edwina muttered to herself as she pawed through her supplies. "These are all getting dull and discolored." She looked up at Tess as she closed the basket's lid and secured it. "I'll get Skippy to take me by the quilt shop later."

"Skip and Milly went to poke around town, Edwina," Tess said. "Skip asked me to tell you they'd be back in time for lunch."

"Okay." She started for the door to put her sewing basket away.

"Edwina," Tess called, "may I have a word with you?"

She turned back. "If this is about Joyce's ridiculous accusations —"

"It has nothing to do with Joyce. It's about Mercy."

Edwina waited, her expression unreadable.

"She called me last night, very upset."

"Mercy's emotional," said Edwina. "She's been in a stew about something ever since I've known her."

"She has reason to be upset this time. Apparently something you said to Wally Tanksley yesterday caused him to give Mercy the brush-off."

"Something I said?" She gave a brittle laugh. "Of course, Mercy would blame me. She always blames me for every unpleasant thing that happens in her miserable life. But I don't even know the man."

"You were talking to him yesterday. I saw you. What did you say to him?"

"I talked to a lot of people yesterday. How am I supposed to remember what I said to all of them?"

"Edwina —"

At that moment, Skip Hector appeared in the doorway. "Aunt Edwina, are you ready for lunch?"

Edwina turned to him with a smile that changed her sour face completely. "Coming, Skippy," she caroled, plainly relieved to get away from Tess and her questions.

Determined not to let Edwina avoid the issue indefinitely, Tess told herself she'd corner her at lunch.

Which turned out to be harder than Tess had anticipated. After filling her own plate, she lingered beside the coffee pot, waiting to see where Edwina would light. Obviously aware that Tess was watching her, Edwina led Skip and Milly to a table where three of the six chairs were already taken by the Bloom sisters and Don Bob Earling.

Later, Tess told herself. Seeing Jenny Vercourt seated alone at a table, Tess joined her. "Where's Willis?" Tess asked.

"He had to go to Springfield after a part for the furnace. If it's not one thing breaking down around here, it's two others. But it'll give him a chance to take his sister to lunch. She's a paralegal there."

"Oh? I've met a couple of Springfield lawyers. What firm is Willis's sister with?"

"Until recently, she worked for one of those firms with a string of names — March, Walker, Something, Something. Anyway, another firm lured her away with a good-sized increase in salary. I'm not sure I ever heard the name of the new firm, Tess. Sorry."

Tess shrugged. "I probably wouldn't know it anyway. There must be dozens of lawyers in Springfield."

Carrying a laden plate in one hand and a tall glass of iced tea in the other, Ross came to a stop beside Jenny. "That woman has taken possesssion of my locker again," he growled.

Jenny looked up at him. "Are you referring to Edwina?"

"Who else? The meanest woman on two legs.

She's confiscated that locker again."

"The one I told her to stay away from yesterday?"

Ross nodded. "Albert let her push him out. That man's got no backbone — but what can you expect from a man who sews?" He watched Jenny, who groaned and put her head in her hands. "Are you going to make her move her stuff again?"

Jenny lifted her head. "I'll handle this, Ross," she said sharply. "You stay out of it."

Ross's brows drew down into a bushy V. "I wasn't going to do anything."

Obviously Jenny didn't believe him. "I mean it, Ross. If you cause another big fuss over that locker, I'll have to bar you from the center for a while."

"Bar me?" he bellowed. "What about Edwina? Are you going to let her have her way about everything?"

"No," Jenny told him, "I'll handle Edwina in my own good time. But you stay out of it."

"I will," Ross snapped. "I'd already decided that locker isn't worth fighting over. I only told you so you'd know what she's done. She should have to obey the rules like everybody else. I sure get told off when I break one. Somebody needs to teach Edwina a lesson." Ross stomped off, cursing under his breath.

"I'll have Willis talk to Edwina tomorrow," Jenny said, turning back to Tess. "Don't you think she'll pay more attention to him than she does to me?"

"I wouldn't bet on it."

"Did I hear Ross correctly? Did he say he wasn't going to fight with Edwina about the locker anymore?"

"That's what he said. Between you and me, I always thought Ross enjoyed fighting with her."

"Me, too. Wonder what's got into him?" Jenny gazed across the cafeteria to where Edwina was seated. "And what am I going to do about Edwina?"

As if aware she was being watched, Edwina looked toward Jenny and Tess, then quickly glanced away.

"I heard Joyce accusing Edwina of having her Mustang towed," Jenny went on.

"Everybody did. Maybe Joyce hoped she'd embarrass Edwina so much she'd pay for the towing."

"Well, it didn't work," Jenny murmured. "Why does Edwina do these things? Doesn't she care what people think of her?"

"I don't believe she does," Tess said, and went on to relate that Mercy suspected Edwina of telling lies about her to Wally Tanksley. "I promised Mercy I'd try to find out what Edwina said to Wally," Tess added, "but she's managed to avoid me all morning."

"I wish Mercy would stand up for herself."

"That's what Luke said last night, but she can't seem to do it, not with Edwina anyway."

"Now even Ross has backed off. It's like

they're all afraid of her," said Jenny, puzzled.

A while later, Tess watched Don Bob Earling get up to help himself to more food then hesitate when Ross did the same. Don Bob waited until Ross had returned to his table before he went to refill his own plate. "I don't think Don Bob's afraid of Ross, but apparently he's still avoiding him like the plague," Tess commented. She went on to tell Jenny about the altercation between the two men during yesterday's book discussion. "I thought Don Bob might have a stroke or something right then and there. I really wanted to kick Ross's butt. What business is it of his if Don Bob is gay?"

"He's not gay."

Tess looked at Jenny, surprised. "How do you know?"

"One day after Ross had taunted him during a card game, Don Bob went to Willis and asked him to talk to Ross. Which Willis did, and you see how much that accomplished. Anyway, Don Bob told Willis that he wasn't gay. He used to be a professional photographer, traveled all over the world for the big magazines like *National Geographic*. He didn't marry during those years because he was out of the country most of the time. Then he contracted some exotic disease in Africa, and he's been impotent ever since."

"Oh, Jenny, that poor man. How terrible."

She sighed. "Yes, it is. Willis said you could tell it almost killed Don Bob to talk about it, but he wanted us to understand how much it hurt for Ross to always be making snide remarks about his never marrying."

"Did Willis tell Ross about Don Bob's problem?"

Jenny shook her head.

"Maybe if he told him . . ."

Jenny shook her head. "I thought of that, but I'm afraid Ross would blurt it out in front of everybody if he got angry with Don Bob."

Upon reflection, Tess thought Jenny could be right. "It would be a lot more pleasant around here if you did bar Ross from the center."

Jenny made a face. "I've been tempted several times, but the government has very strict rules about discrimination, and I'm sure Ross could make a good case for himself."

"Hmmm," Tess agreed. "He'd probably portray himself as the long-suffering victim of male discrimination by the female majority."

Jenny laughed. "Poor mistreated man."

Later, as the seniors left the cafeteria, Tess saw her chance to speak to Edwina. Skip and Milly had gone ahead to the rec room, while Edwina had stayed behind to get her covered dish.

Tess walked up behind the other woman before Edwina knew she was there. "Edwina, I want to talk to you."

Edwina jumped and turned, clutching the foil-covered dish to her chest. "Not now, Tess.

I'm not feeling well." And indeed, she did look a little pale, but Tess felt no sympathy. This was probably just another one of Edwina's tricks.

"It'll only take a few minutes, Edwina."

Edwina shook her head, backing off. "It'll have to wait, Tess. I feel like I'm going to throw up." She moved around the table, and clapping one hand over her mouth, ran from the room.

Tess didn't know if Edwina really was sick or if the upset stomach was just an excuse to get away. And by the time Tess had helped Jenny clean up, Edwina had left the center with her nephew and his wife.

8

Late that afternoon, Tess returned to Iris House. Milly and Skip hadn't come in yet. Perhaps they'd stayed with Edwina or were downtown. Since few tourists were in Victoria Springs in February, it was a good time to visit the shops. Tess hoped the young couple had gone somewhere together and were enjoying themselves. From their conversation at breakfast, Tess knew that Milly, at least, thought it was about time.

More to the point, if the Hectors had dropped Edwina off at her house and left, then Edwina was alone.

Tess dialed Edwina's number and let the phone ring ten times, but there was no answer. Surely Skip and Milly hadn't taken Edwina on their outing. Tess reflected upon it and decided that more probably Edwina was at home and not answering her phone for fear it was Tess or Joyce calling to badger her. Imagining Edwina sitting there wearing a smug smile, surrounded by her accumulated junk, while the phone rang and rang, roused Tess's ire.

She called Edwina's house several times

during the next hour, but still there was no answer, which nudged Tess's impatience a few notches higher.

Well, she could be as determined as Edwina. She got her coat and went out to her car. She would go to Edwina's house and plant herself on Edwina's porch until the woman let her in.

Every time Tess drove down Edwina's block of small frame houses, she marveled, as with fresh eyes, at the sharp contrast between Edwina's home and the others on the block. None of the neighboring houses had peeling paint or leaning fences. None had stalks of dead weeds in the yard or clumps of dead castor beans that had fallen over and covered most of the walk. The neatness of the other houses made Edwina's shabby property even more noticeable. It was like a big smear of ugly black grease on a white dress.

Perhaps Edwina was too strapped to do anything about it, Tess thought, as she pulled into Edwina's cracked and crumbling driveway and noticed the red Honda was not in sight. Skip and Milly must have dropped Edwina off, then gone somewhere together. For a moment, pity almost doused Tess's indignation. Edwina was alone, without friends, and from appearances she was struggling very hard to make ends meet. But then Tess reminded herself that whatever Edwina's problems were they didn't give her the right to trample all over people who were too weak or too kind to stop her.

She got out of the car and climbed the front steps to the porch, where a wood plank gave slightly when she stepped on it. She jumped to another spot, peering down at the offending plank. It was rotting along one side. Eventually somebody was going to step right through it and injure themselves if Edwina didn't have it replaced. Tess made a mental note to avoid it as she left.

She went to the door, knocked, and called Edwina's name. The door remained closed, and she heard no movement inside. Tess knocked again, and again got no response. She bent over to peer into a front window, but a stack of old magazines blocked her view of the interior. She went back to the door and knocked again.

Either Edwina was not at home or she wasn't going to show herself, no matter how long Tess waited. Finally admitting defeat, Tess turned away. But then she thought she heard a noise from inside the house. She turned back and called, "Edwina?"

There it was again. A sound like a muffled moan. Tess opened the sagging screen door and twisted the doorknob. The door creaked open. Taking a few cautious steps inside, she halted to let her eyes adjust to the dimness.

"Edwina."

Another moaning sound. It came from somewhere to Tess's left. Tess found a light switch just inside the door and flipped it on. A single ceiling bulb cast an eerie yellow glow over the piles of trash surrounding Tess and the narrow, dark pathway leading through the room.

Tess followed the path, which took her to a hallway. She could see a cabinet with a faucet over it in the room opposite — the kitchen. The low moaning seemed to be coming from there. When she stepped into the kitchen, the sour smell of vomit assailed her. Covering her mouth and nose with her hand, she flipped on the light.

Edwina Riley was slumped, half-sitting, half-lying, in a corner. Her head hung to one side, and she'd vomited on the floor.

"Edwina!" Tess rushed to her.

Edwina groaned and peered at her with wild, red-streaked eyes. "Skippy?"

"No, it's Tess Darcy, Edwina." She grasped Edwina's arm, intending to help her up, but the woman made no effort to rise. She was a dead weight. When Tess realized how clammy and cold Edwina's skin was, she decided it was better not to move her after all.

Edwina groaned. "Is that you, Tess?"

"Yes, it's me."

"I — I was trying to get to the phone to call somebody, but it's so far — and I — I kept vomiting — ohhh. . . ." She began to retch again, racking dry heaves.

Tess rummaged in a cabinet drawer and found a torn piece of dish towel. She wet it at the sink and used it to wipe Edwina's pale face and then to clean up the worst of the mess on the floor. She held her breath until she'd disposed of the vomit-soaked rag in the trash can that stood in a corner. She found another towel, wet it, and pressed it against Edwina's brow.

"I told Skip I wasn't feeling well, but Milly kept whining about wanting him to spend time with her. So they left me alone, and me as sick as a dog." Her head lolled back against the wall and she seemed so exhausted that even breathing was an effort. Finally she said, "It wasn't Skippy's fault. It was her."

"I'm sure she wasn't being deliberately thoughtless. They are on their honeymoon."

Suddenly, Edwina groaned and doubled over with pain.

Tess looked around for a phone. "Where do you hurt, Edwina?"

"Stomach," Edwina gasped, "guts — everywhere. I — I've never been so sick in my life. I think Ross poisoned me."

Stunned by the accusation, Tess whirled to stare at Edwina, whose head lolled back against the wall again. Holding it upright appeared to be more than she could manage.

"Why do you think Ross poisoned you, Edwina?"

"He — he was mad because Albert let me have my locker back. Ross said somebody ought to neu-neutralize me, that's what he said. But I think he meant kill me."

"He probably meant he was going to report you to Jenny. He didn't mention poison, did he?"

She raised her head with an effort. "No" — her voice was an urgent whisper now — "but he meant to hurt me. I'm sure of it."

Her head fell back against the wall again with a thump. She expelled a harsh breath and closed her eyes.

With rising alarm, Tess saw that what remained of the vomit on the floor was blood-streaked. Edwina was desperately ill. She had to get help for her fast. She glanced around, wondering where in all the mess there might be a telephone. "Edwina, where's your phone?"

Edwina didn't answer.

Tess gripped her shoulder, shook her gently. "Edwina, answer me! Where's your phone?"

Edwina's eyelids fluttered and she muttered something that sounded like "kitchen."

But they were in the kitchen, and Tess couldn't see a phone. Then she noticed a small table in one corner covered with old rags and other discards. She began grabbing things and throwing them off and at last uncovered the phone. She dialed 911 and gave Edwina's address. "It's urgent," Tess said. "She's very ill. Please hurry."

She hung up and went back to kneel beside Edwina. She touched her brow. "Hold on, Edwina. Help's coming. You're going to be all right."

Edwina did not respond. She'd lost consciousness.

A few minutes later, Tess heard the ambulance siren. She ran to the front door and threw it open. A medic bolted from each side of the ambulance, dashed to the back, and pulled out a stretcher.

"Hurry!" Tess cried as they reached the front steps, even though the men were running by then.

"Whoa," cried the first medic as he reached the door and saw the piles of newspapers and magazines. "What's all this?"

Tess had an illogical urge to defend Edwina. "Ms. Riley is a collector," she said impatiently. "This way." She led them to the kitchen and stood aside as they checked Edwina's vital signs, fitted her with an oxygen mask, loaded her on the stretcher, and hurried out.

"You can check on her at the emergency room, ma'am," one of the medics called back as they went out the door.

He probably assumed Tess was a relative. Tess debated, then decided that instead of going directly to the hospital, she should find Skip and Milly. Edwina would want Skip there when she regained consciousness.

If she regained consciousness. Determinedly Tess banished that thought.

She recalled Ross's complaint to Jenny at lunch, his saying that somebody needed to teach Edwina a lesson. But poison? Tess shook off that thought, too. Edwina hadn't been completely rational when she uttered that accusation.

She decided to go back to Iris House first to see if the Hectors had returned. If not, she'd scour the business district.

With a wave of relief, Tess saw the red Honda parked at the curb when she arrived home. She slammed out of the car and ran all the way into the house and up the stairs to the Annabel Jane Room.

Tess heard the shower running even before Skip opened the door. He was wearing gray sweats and thick, white athletic socks. And his eyes were puffy, as though he'd been asleep when she knocked. "Skip," Tess blurted and paused to gasp for breath. "Your aunt's been taken to the hospital. She's very ill."

For an instant, Skip just stared at her, as if he'd suddenly gone into a trance. Then he blinked and rubbed his eyes with the heels of his hands. "Did you say Aunt Edwina is sick?"

"Very sick."

"Is it her heart?"

"I don't know, Skip. But when I went to her house, I found her too ill to get to the telephone. I called an ambulance. She was unconscious when the medics arrived. They've taken her to the emergency room. Frankly, I'm a little frightened for her, Skip. You should get there right away."

He finally seemed to grasp the urgency in her tone. Leaving the door ajar, he grabbed a pair of white athletic shoes off the dresser and sat on the side of the bed to put them on. "I guess

I should wait for Milly. She's in the shower."

"You go on," Tess said. "I'll tell Milly what's happened and bring her to the hospital when she's ready."

He snatched a ring of keys from the dresser and started out the door, coatless. Then he turned back. "I don't even know where the hospital is."

Tess gave him directions, adding, "Won't you need a coat?"

He shook his head. "I'll be all right." He ran out again and bounded down the stairs. Tess heard the shower go off. She went to the closed bathroom door and tapped. "Milly, it's Tess Darcy. I need to talk to you."

9

When Tess and Milly reached the emergency room, Skip was slumped on a leather couch, his elbows on his knees and his head in his hands. A man in a green surgical scrub suit sat beside him. The man was bent toward Skip, talking quietly.

Milly rushed to Skip. "How's Edwina?"

Both men looked up. "This is Dr. Blane, Milly. My fi—" Skip looked past Milly and saw Tess behind her. "Er . . . my wife, Milly. And this is Tess Darcy. We're staying at her bed and breakfast."

Hands were shaken, hellos exchanged.

Skip came slowly to his feet. "She's gone, Milly. Aunt Edwina's dead." He reached blindly for her. "I didn't even get to talk to her before . . . before . . ." His voice trailed off.

Milly froze for a moment, staring at Skip with her mouth half-open. Then she seemed to shake herself as she put her arms around him and patted his back comfortingly.

Finally Milly released Skip and turned to the doctor. "She wasn't feeling very well when we took her home today. She said she was feeling nauseated, but I never thought . . ." She looked down. "I told her to take a nap and she'd feel better. I just wanted to get away." She drew in a shaky breath. "Skip told me she had a bad heart, but I never even thought of it. Oh, God, if I'd known . . ."

"I'm not sure it was her heart," Dr. Blane said.

Skip's expression was puzzled. "Then, what?"

"We have to run some tests. When had she eaten last?"

Milly and Skip exchanged a baffled look, and so Tess answered the doctor. "Today at noon. We all ate at the senior citizens center. It was a covered-dish luncheon."

The doctor's brow creased. "Is anyone else sick?"

"I don't know," Tess said. "The three of us" — she indicated Skip and Milly — "ate there, and we're fine. I — I could call around, find out if any of the others is sick."

"It sounds like you're suggesting Edwina might have died of food poisoning, doctor," Milly said.

"From her symptoms, it's a possibility. We pumped her stomach and will test what we got, but she'd pretty well gotten rid of everything before she reached the hospital."

"I think she'd vomited repeatedly by the time I found her," Tess said.

"You found her?" Dr. Blane asked.

"Yes. She didn't answer her door, and I was leaving when I heard her moaning."

"Was she still conscious? Did she say anything?"

Tess swallowed hard. "Only that she'd never been so sick in her life, that she hurt everywhere. She seemed a little disoriented. At first, she thought I was her nephew." And she accused Ross Dellin of poisoning her, but Tess would keep that to herself for now. "A couple of times before she lost consciousness, she doubled over with pain in her stomach."

The doctor nodded thoughtfully.

Milly, who'd seemed absorbed in her own thoughts, asked, "How soon will you know the cause of death?"

"The pathologist can probably do the autopsy tomorrow. We should get the results of some of the tests by the next day."

"I'll go home and start making those phone calls," Tess said.

"If anyone else is sick, tell them to get to the hospital right away," the doctor said.

Tess nodded. The doctor's clear concern caused a new frisson of alarm to run through Tess. She left Skip and Milly talking to Dr. Blane. Skip was asking about funeral homes and if they'd pick up the body. The doctor suggested that he might want to spend a few moments with his aunt alone.

Skip declined and returned to the disposition of the body. He appeared to be worried about the funeral arrangements. To Tess, his eagerness to get Edwina into the ground seemed inappropriate so soon after the death. But then people reacted to shock in different ways.

Back at Iris House, Tess called Jenny Vercourt and told her the news, adding, "They'll do an autopsy, but the doctor suspects Edwina was poisoned."

"Poisoned!"

"Yes, he wanted to know if anybody else who ate at the potluck had gotten sick."

"Willis and I are fine and evidently so are you," Jenny said.

"Right, and Skip and Milly aren't sick, either. But I promised I'd try to contact everybody else who was there."

"I can help," Jenny said. "I'll check on the McBrooms, Mercy, and the Bloom sisters."

"Thank you, Jenny. I'll get in touch with Joyce, Ross, and Don Bob. Is that all?"

Jenny was silent for a moment. "I think so, yes."

"Maybe I'll call Wally Tanksley, too. He wasn't at the potluck, but he talked to Edwina for quite a while the day before. He should know what's happened."

An hour later, Tess had reached everybody on her list. They all felt fine and seemed thoroughly shocked to hear of Edwina's death.

"I thought she was too mean to die" was Ross's reaction. Would he say something like that if he'd poisoned her? Tess had to admit that she wasn't sure what Ross might say or do.

"Ross, before she died, Edwina told me you'd poisoned her."

"What?"

"She told me you said she should be neutralized."

"Oh. Yeah, I did say that, but that's a helluva long way from poisoning her. Good God, what made her say a thing like that?"

"I don't know," Tess admitted. "She was in a lot of pain and lost consciousness moments later."

"Must've been out of her head," Ross said. Tess hung up, thinking that he didn't sound like a man who had killed someone and was fearful of getting caught. She reminded herself that the doctor suspected food poisoning, which, if the cause, would seem to eliminate murder.

Her next call was to Joyce Banaker, who sounded more upset over not being able to collect the ninety-dollar towing fee than over her neighbor's unexpected demise. In fact, she voiced her hope that somebody with some pride would buy Edwina's house and clean it up.

Don Bob Earling just sounded bumfuzzled and kept saying, "But she was her usual irascible self at the center today."

Wally Tanksley expressed his regret but said he hadn't really known Edwina.

Clearly there wouldn't be many mourners at Edwina's funeral.

Tess touched base with Jenny later and learned that nobody on Jenny's list was sick, either. If Edwina had gotten food poisoning at the potluck, then she must have eaten something nobody else ate. Neither Jenny nor Tess could think what that might be.

"Maybe it was something she ate at home before she got here," Jenny suggested.

"Could be," Tess agreed. "But she'd thrown up everything in her stomach, so we may never know what it was." But what if Edwina had been poisoned — murdered — Tess asked herself as she hung up. Immediately her mind flew to Skip. Instead of expressing grief at the hospital over his aunt's death, he'd been inordinately concerned with getting Edwina buried. Also, she'd overheard Skip admit to Milly that he expected to inherit something from his aunt. He knew she had a bad heart, but people had survived for years with bad hearts. Had Skip decided to make sure Edwina didn't?

Tess was not the only one pondering that question. At Edwina's house, Skip was going through every drawer in a frenzy and muttering, "Damn, damn, damn! Her lawyer's name has to be here somewhere." He was a man possessed.

Milly had been watching this incredible performance for the past ten minutes, wishing she could read his mind. Ever since they'd talked to the doctor at the hospital, she'd been asking herself why Skip was so anxious to get Edwina buried. Furthermore, why had he been so eager to come to Victoria Springs at this particular time. She also kept remembering that he said he didn't think Edwina would live much longer, that she had one foot in the grave.

"What's the big hurry?" Milly asked finally.

Throwing up his hands in frustration, he spun away from the dresser he'd been ransacking in Edwina's bedroom. "I have to contact her lawyer. He'll have a copy of the will. I can't find one around here. Maybe she kept it in a safe-deposit box somewhere."

"Did you ever think that perhaps she never made a will? Lawyers cost money, and so do safe-deposit boxes. You know how tight she was. Maybe she's been lying to you about the will."

Skip paused to rake his hair out of his eyes and looked reflective. "Without a will, I'm her only heir. Which would be a good thing, in one way. On the other hand, if there's no will, it could take longer for me to get possession of my inheritance."

He sounded frustrated but otherwise as cool as a cucumber, as if he were talking about some irritating problem with the IRS. How could she have lived with this man close to a year without ever seeing this side of him? She'd known he was lazy and manipulative, but not that he was unfeeling, even cruel — until now. "I never realized what a cold bastard you are, Skip."

He gazed at her for an instant, then lifted his shoulders in a shrug. "Give me a break, Milly. I'm just being realistic. It's not as if I was all that close to Aunt Edwina. And she's dead now; there's nothing I can do about that."

"But you're glad, aren't you?"

His eyes narrowed. "That hurts, Milly. I can't believe you'd say such a thing."

She persisted. "How did you know she was going to die, Skip?"

His brow furrowed. He looked bewildered. "I didn't know. How could I?"

"You told me she had one foot in the grave. You said she couldn't live much longer."

The furrows eased. "Oh. I just meant that she was old. Old people die all the time."

She let that pass. "And for the rest of us, life goes on, right?"

"Yeah, that's right," he said with a frown of irritation. "Why are you being so critical all of a sudden? You know how much I need my inheritance, Milly. I wish I knew how soon I could get it."

"I wouldn't say things like that to anybody else," she advised.

"What, I'm not supposed to speak the truth? I need that money. To start with, there will be the funeral costs."

Milly told herself to stop imagining things. It was pure coincidence that Edwina had died during their visit. And Skip was right to want to get the estate settled as quickly as possible. “Maybe you can have access to her checking account.”

His shoulders slumped. “I found her checkbook. It’s got a balance of less than two hundred dollars. Even if I could get to it, that sure as hell won’t pay for a funeral.”

“Well, don’t look at me,” Milly said. “We’ve about maxed out my credit cards since you’ve been out of work. Maybe the funeral home will wait for their money until you can sell the house.”

“Not likely.” He bent over and began pawing through a bottom dresser drawer, then finally started throwing out small rolls of paper secured tightly with rubber bands. “Look at this. She kept every check she ever wrote. There’s a year’s worth in each of these rolls. What was she thinking? Was she nuts?”

“She just couldn’t throw anything away,” Milly said. “If that’s crazy, then she was crazy.”

Edwina’s bedroom was the one room in the house without stacks of junk in every available space. The cement-block-and-plank shelves along two walls were crammed full of everything but books — as Edwina had repeatedly said, she didn’t have money to spend on books. Otherwise the room was relatively uncluttered.

Now the small rolls of checks Skip had been throwing from the dresser drawer were all over the floor and the bed, and he continued to throw out more of them. When he had emptied the drawer, he sagged on a corner of the mattress. "There's probably a check to her lawyer in there somewhere." He shoved check rolls out of the way and flopped down on his back on the bed. "It could take us all night to find it."

"Us? I don't think so."

He looked over at her. "What's that mean?"

"It means I'm not going to spend the night looking through cancelled checks. If you want to, be my guest. I'm leaving. Call me at Iris House when you're finished here."

"Milly!" he wailed as she left the bedroom. But she didn't look back. At the moment, she didn't want to see Skip. She was having trouble shutting off her suspicions. She had to get out of there, find some place where she could be alone and think.

Was it mere coincidence that Edwina had died while they were in Victoria Springs?

She wanted desperately to believe it was coincidence because to think otherwise was terrifying.

But the nagging questions wouldn't leave her alone. Prior to his decision to come to Victoria Springs, Skip hadn't seemed at all concerned about his aunt. In fact, he'd hardly mentioned her in the past year. As he'd said himself, they weren't close. Then, all of a sudden, they had to visit her. Immediately. It couldn't wait. He couldn't give Milly a good reason, but it was important. She was just supposed to take his word for it and get with the program like a good girl.

That first night in bed, he'd actually been toting up the sum of his inheritance — or what he hoped the total might be. It was possible, Milly mused, that it had been more than hope. Skip could recently have found out that Edwina had a savings account and how much was in it. If the account actually contained several thousand dollars, as he'd suggested, it would explain his sudden plan to butter up Edwina by visiting and find out what he could about her will while he was there. He might even have imagined he could tap her for a loan. But had that been all that was on Skip's mind?

Looking back on it now, Milly thought again that it was as if Skip had insisted on coming to Victoria Springs because he'd known Edwina was going to die.

10

The next day at the senior citizens center, Tess asked the people who'd stayed for the potluck luncheon to write down everything they'd eaten. When the lists were compared, it seemed that several people had eaten from every dish that was brought, with the single exception of Edwina's macaroni and cheese.

"Maybe the food poisoning was in that," Don Bob suggested.

"Edwina never eats what she brings," Mercy said with a sad little smile that was gone almost as quickly as it appeared.

"Can't blame her," snorted Ross, then had the good grace to duck his head when he remembered he was speaking of the dead. But he recovered quickly and glared around at the accusing eyes fixed on him, "Well, it's the truth, so you people can stop looking at me like I've just desecrated a grave or something. That stuff Edwina brought wasn't fit for a dog."

"I'm sure she didn't eat any of her own food yesterday," Joyce put in. "I saw what she had on her plate. It looked like she'd taken a little of everything else but her macaroni and cheese."

"Could she have eaten some of it after she got home?" Anita asked.

"I doubt it," Tess said. "She was already feeling unwell when she left the center, and Milly says Edwina was complaining about being nauseated when they dropped her off at her house." Nevertheless, she'd tell Skip and Milly not to eat any of the dish, if they found it in Edwina's refrigerator. If Skip was responsible for Edwina's death, he'd already know what to avoid, of course. She thought about it for a moment. "If Edwina was poisoned, I don't think the food was responsible." She looked around at the group gathered at a couple of tables in the dining room. "We've just proved it. Collectively we sampled everything that was on the table yesterday — except for the macaroni and cheese — and none of us suffered a twinge of discomfort."

"Well, I hope they find out soon what did cause Edwina's death," Jenny said, distractedly raking back a lock of brown hair. She looked exhausted, as if she hadn't slept at all last night. "I know it sounds crass to mention this before the poor woman's even buried, but if rumors get out that Edwina died of food poisoning after eating here, the state health department could shut us down."

"We can't let that happen!" cried Mercy.

"For sure," said Anita. "Albert and I so look forward to the activities here. What would we all do without the center?"

Jenny smiled wanly. "Thanks, Anita. For what it's worth, Willis says I borrow trouble, but I can't help worrying about this."

"It would be worse if that meal had come out of your kitchen, Jenny," Albert pointed out. "But we'll all talk to the health department if they give you any problems. They can't blame it on that meal if we swear that among us we ate everything that Edwina did."

Hattie Bloom reached across the table and patted Jenny's hand. "He's right, Jenny."

"It could have been her heart," Mercy said hopefully. "She had a flare-up a couple of years ago."

"We won't learn anything by speculating," Joyce said. "I think I'll go and do some quilting. At times like this it's best to keep busy."

"Don Bob," Ross said, "how about a game of dominoes?"

If this was an olive branch, Don Bob wasn't taking it. "No, thanks," he said curtly. "They've been showing reruns of the Andy Griffith show on Channel 20. Think I'll go and see which one's on today." With the aid of his cane, Don Bob pushed himself to his feet and hobbled out.

Ross frowned at Don Bob's back, but the usual derisive retort was not forthcoming. Even Ross seemed subdued by the unexpected death of his principal sparring partner.

Still looking troubled, Jenny excused herself,

saying that she needed to get back to the kitchen.

As the others left the dining room, most of them to join the quilting circle, Tess gazed after them pensively.

Even though she had said she didn't believe Edwina had been poisoned by what she had eaten at the covered-dish luncheon, there remained one possibility nobody had mentioned. She couldn't help wondering if Skip or another of the people who'd been at the pot-luck luncheon — Ross, for example — had somehow added the poison to Edwina's food after it was on her plate.

Tess closed her eyes and recalled what she could of Edwina's movements in the lunch room yesterday. Edwina had been close to the last in line to serve herself from the covered dishes. Tess had been paying closer attention than usual because she was still trying to get Edwina alone to talk to her on Mercy's behalf. Skip and Milly had been in front of Edwina in the line, but Tess couldn't remember either of them — or anybody else — being close enough to Edwina to have put something in her food as she was filling her plate.

Then Skip, Milly, and Edwina had sat at a table where three other people were already seated. Concentrating, Tess finally remembered who the other three diners were. The Bloom sisters and Don Bob Earling.

Tess didn't see how any of the other five

people at the table could have added anything to Edwina's food without somebody else noticing. Besides, why would Hattie or Opal or Don Bob have wanted to poison Edwina? Considering Edwina's contentious nature, everybody at the center had probably exchanged a few cross words with her at one time or another, but Tess could not remember any serious disagreements between Edwina and any of those three. On the other hand, Edwina had had angry run-ins with Ross, Mercy, Joyce, and the McBrooms. Yet as far as Tess could recall, none of them had been anywhere near Edwina's food after she'd put it on her plate.

Skip and Milly had been seated on either side of Edwina at lunch yesterday. It was possible, but only remotely possible, that one of them could have dropped something in Edwina's food — say, while reaching for a salt shaker — without one of the other diners at the table noticing. But what a risk to take, when they could have much more easily added poison to food at Edwina's house.

Thinking of the Hectors reminded Tess that, just to be safe, she needed to caution them about the macaroni and cheese. She used the phone in the office to call the Annabel Jane Room at Iris House. When she explained to Milly what she wanted, Milly said, "It's okay, Tess. Skip cleaned out the refrigerator last night, threw everything away so he could defrost it."

Fast work, Tess thought as she hung up. Skip wasn't letting any grass grow under his feet. She stared out the window. As difficult as it was for Tess to see the young couple as murderers, she kept remembering the breakfast conversation she'd overheard yesterday. Skip had said something about making headway with Edwina. To which Milly had responded that she was tired of waiting around while Skip talked his aunt into leaving everything she had to him when she died. Milly had suggested the inheritance would be only a few hundred dollars, but perhaps Skip knew it was more than that.

Upon consideration, though, Tess tended to agree with Milly. If Edwina had sizable savings, she would surely have spent some of it on the much-needed repairs to her house.

Shaking off these thoughts, Tess went to the kitchen to see if she could help Jenny with lunch, telling herself that the possibility remained that Edwina had not died of poisoning at all. And they wouldn't know for sure until the medical examiner reported his findings.

"I'm out of milk and flour," Jenny said, when Tess asked what she could do. "Could you possibly run to the store for me?"

"I'm on my way," Tess told her.

As it turned out, any remaining doubt Tess had that Edwina was murdered was banished when the following day, Friday, Chief of Police

Desmond Butts showed up at the center shortly after noon. He stepped into the dining room, where lunch was in progress, and his piercing gaze swept the diners.

Jenny was the first to notice Butts, a second before he cleared his throat portentously.

Hastily Jenny pushed her chair back and walked over to him. "Chief Butts, I didn't hear you come in." She extended a hand. "I'm the director of the center, Jenny Vercourt. You may not remember, but my husband and I met you at a Lions Club dinner last year."

Bushy-headed and spectacled, Butts tilted his ruddy, blunt-featured face to squint down at Jenny. "I remember," he growled. Tess noticed that as usual Butts appeared to be in a bad mood. Then Butts saw Tess, and a slow dawning of resignation came over his face as he sent a faint nod in her direction. By now everybody had stopped eating and all eyes were on the chief.

"May I help you, Chief Butts?" Jenny prompted.

A muscle in Butts's square jaw twitched as he returned his gaze to Jenny. "I hope so, Miz Vercourt, I surely do."

"Shall we go into my office?"

Butts scanned the room again, his eyes stopping at Tess's face. She held his look without blinking, and he sniffed and moved on. Finally he said, "Nope. I want to talk to all these people — that is, everybody who was here day before yesterday, the day Edwina Riley died. How many is that?"

Hesitantly Joyce Banaker raised her hand. Then Albert McBroom's hand went up, and finally all the diners put their hands in the air.

Butts extended an index finger and counted. "That's nine of you. Anybody else present that day who's not here now?"

The diners looked around. Jenny said, "My husband was here. He's out back, cleaning up a vacant apartment, getting it ready to rent."

"Well, go get him," Butts commanded. As Jenny hurried from the room, the Chief extracted a small tablet and pen from his uniform pocket. "Are we missing anybody else?" he inquired of the group.

Tess cleared her throat. "Edwina's nephew and his wife ate with us that day. Skip and Milly Hector. They're on their honeymoon, staying at Iris House."

Butts's bushy brows shot up, and he gave her a narrow look. "Why am I not surprised?" he muttered and sighed heavily. "And what, may I ask, are you doing here, Tess? You haven't made enough money off Iris House to retire already, have you?"

Butts's efforts at humor always fell flat with Tess. She lifted her chin and frowned at him. It wasn't her fault that she'd somehow been involved in a few of Butts's previous murder investigations. "I'm a volunteer at the center this month. I didn't expect to have any guests at all at Iris House until March, but then the Hectors came."

Butts studied her for another moment, mumbled something under his breath, then shrugged. "Okay. First I'm gonna need everybody's name, address, and phone number."

While Butts was writing the information in his tablet, Jenny came back with Willis and they slid quietly into two chairs at an unoccupied table. Tess glanced around the room. Joyce appeared alert and curious, studying each person as he or she gave Butts the requested data. Ross shifted restlessly in his seat and watched Butts warily. Mercy's nervous fingers folded and refolded her paper napkin. Hattie and Opal had their heads together, whispering softly and from time to time shaking their heads as though bewildered by what was happening. The others looked down at their hands or at their food, which would be stone-cold by the time they got around to eating, but they all seemed to have lost their appetite anyway.

It was Ross who finally asked the question that must have been on everybody's mind. "What's this all about, Chief? We've already determined that everything Edwina ate that day was eaten by some of the rest of us, and we didn't get sick."

"Miz Riley didn't die of food poisoning."

Mercy's fingers abruptly stopped fiddling with her napkin and her head shot up. "Oh, it was her heart, after all," she cried. She looked vastly relieved.

"No, ma'am. It wasn't food poisoning, but it was poison, all right."

11

It was Joyce who finally broke the shocked silence. "Are you suggesting that one of us added poison to Edwina's food while she was eating?" Joyce was giving voice to the thought that had been going through Tess's mind for the past twenty-four hours.

Everybody else turned to stare at Joyce in surprise, as if the idea had not occurred to them.

"No, ma'am," Butts said, "but that's an interesting idea." He glanced around the room. Nobody met his eyes. He went on, "That's not how it happened, though. They didn't find poison in her stomach or intestines. But there was a highly toxic poison in her blood." He flipped to the back of his tablet and pronounced slowly, "Ricinus communis, also called ricin."

The diners exchanged puzzled looks.

"What's that?" Mercy queried weakly.

"Never heard of it," Ross blustered, as if offended by the mention of something he had no knowledge of. Tess scrutinized his face, remembering Edwina's words:

I think he meant to kill me. Ross poisoned me.

Was Ross's proclaimed ignorance of the poison that had killed Edwina merely an act?

Willis spoke up. "Wait a minute. If Edwina didn't get the poison in something she ate, how did she get it?"

"Like I said," Butts replied impatiently, "it was in her blood. According to the doc, it got there through her skin some way."

Hattie Bloom frowned in bewilderment. "You mean it was injected, like with a hypodermic needle?"

Murmurs of amazement ran through the group. "That's impossible," Ross pronounced. "If somebody tried to give Edwina a shot, she'd have bellowed loud enough to be heard all over town."

"They didn't find any breaks in her skin that looked like they were made by a hypodermic needle," Butts said.

"Then how the hell did the poison get in her blood?" Don Bob asked, scowling, as impatient as Ross seemed to be.

"It could've gone through any opening in her skin, like a cut." Butts stared around the room, as if expecting somebody to volunteer further information.

Nobody did.

Butts scratched his head. "I want to talk to every one of you alone." He glanced toward the table where Jenny and Willis sat. "I'll need someplace private to conduct the interviews."

"You can use the office," Jenny said. "It's through that door, next to the game room."

Butts nodded. "Okay. Who wants to be first?"

"I will," Willis said. "I need to get back to work."

During the next hour, each person took his turn with Butts in the office. Joyce Banaker was third to be interviewed. When she returned to the dining room, she was disgruntled. "That man is downright insulting," she confided to Tess, who'd had enough exchanges with Butts to know that his interrogation technique was far from gentle. Since he often worked alone, there was no good-guy, bad-guy routine such as you saw on television. Butts was always the bad guy.

"What did he say to you?" Tess asked.

"He wanted to know if I'd ever had a disagreement with Edwina." She rolled her eyes. "I was tempted to ask him if the sun ever came up in the east, but I didn't, of course. I just said that almost everybody who knew Edwina had disagreed with her over something. Then he wanted me to gossip about the others."

Was it only two days ago that Joyce had vowed to make Edwina pay her the ninety dollars for the towing bill? *I'm tired of being harassed. It's finished. I'll see to that, whatever it takes.*

"It's not exactly gossiping, Joyce," Tess

pointed out. “He’s looking for motives.”

“Well, I don’t care! He made me mad. I told him about the dirty tricks Edwina played on me, reporting every slight infraction of regulations to the city and having my Mustang towed. I refuse to sugarcoat Edwina’s meanness just because she’s dead. But I’d bite my tongue off before I’d give that man information about anybody else. I said he’d have to ask the others about their problems with Edwina.”

An admirable posture, Tess thought, but she doubted that the others would follow suit. Don Bob would be only too glad to report on Ross’s and Edwina’s skirmishes. And Ross would probably fill Butts in on everybody else’s dealings with Edwina.

Tess was the last to face Butts in the center’s little cubbyhole of an office. The fake walnut desk and Butts, looming in the chair behind it, took up most of the space. The only other chair in the room faced Butts across the desk, and Tess took it.

Butts leaned back, causing his chair to creak ominously, and linked his hands behind his head. “Beats the hell outta me how you keep turning up when people get murdered, Tess.”

“It’s bad luck.”

His lips twisted in what was Butts’s version of a wry smile. “Or some kind of instinct that makes your scalp prickle when somebody’s about to get offed.” He watched Tess for a reaction.

"Chief, if I'd had any idea that one of the senior citizens was going to die at the center, believe me I'd have found somewhere else to volunteer my time."

"Uh-huh," Butts said with a tinge of disbelief, then continued, "Well, seems like we've got us a regular hotbed of intrigue around here."

So Ross, or somebody, had filled him in on Edwina's differences with the other seniors. But Tess wondered what he meant by "we" and said, "They have their disagreements, like any other group of people who spend a lot of time together."

He sat forward in his chair and glanced over the notes he'd taken. "Let's see, we've got Ross Dellin threatening to kill Miz Riley and throwing her stuff out of her locker." He looked at Tess. "You think he did it?"

"He and Edwina argued a lot. They acted like a couple of little kids." Tess hesitated, thinking, then decided she had to report Edwina's dying accusation. "Chief, when I found Edwina at her house, she said that Ross had poisoned her."

His eyebrows shot up. "Really? Well, we may just wrap this thing up today —"

Tess held up a cautionary hand. "Let me finish. When I pressed Edwina, she admitted that what Ross had really said was that she should be neutralized. He was mad about her claiming one of the center's lockers that he considered his."

"I can't believe all the fuss was over a locker."

"I told you they were like two children. Frankly, if Ross ever resorted to murder — and I'm not saying he did — it's much more likely it would be an impulse killing, a lashing out in anger. Ross has a hot temper, but would he poison someone?" She shook her head doubtfully.

Butts wrote something beside Ross's name. "I'll get back to Dellin later." He consulted his notes again. "Let's see here. Seems like a lot of people had it in for Miz Riley. We got Mercy Bates in tears because the victim said something unflattering about her to her boyfriend." Again he looked up at Tess. "What'd Miz Riley say, do you know?"

"No. Mercy asked me to find out, which I tried to do several times the day of the potluck, but Edwina refused to talk to me about it. Perhaps Wally Tanksley will tell you."

"That's the boyfriend?"

Tess nodded.

He flipped to a clean page in his tablet and made a note. Then he returned to his previous scribbling. "We've got Joyce Banaker yelling at Riley that she's going to make her pay for a ninety-dollar towing bill and Anita and Albert McBroom avoiding Riley like she was a rabid dog. Nobody seems to know what that's about." He gazed at Tess with the unspoken question hanging in the air between them.

"I don't know, either," Tess said. "Honestly, I've only been here for a couple of weeks. Almost anybody else here knows more about the McBrooms — and the others — than I do."

Butts waved a beefy hand. "If they do, they didn't tell me. But I'll bet you could find out."

Tess eyed him suspiciously. Butts asking for her help? What was this? "Maybe."

"All the McBrooms would say was that Miz Riley was a troublemaker, not the sort of person they cared to associate with."

Tess nodded, recalling the conversation about Edwina between the McBrooms outside the sewing room.

What was it Albert had said when Anita had asked how long they had to put up with Edwina? *You know the answer to that. . . . Till we're dead — or she is.* The words came back to Tess now with an ominous ring. But people exaggerated all the time in speech. That didn't make them murderers. She would talk to Anita and Albert and see if she could find out what was behind that conversation before she reported it to Butts.

The Chief glanced at his tablet once more. "Even Jenny Vercourt admitted she often wished the victim would stop coming to the center because she caused so much upheaval."

"Jenny could have told her not to come back. She didn't have to kill her, if that's what you're implying."

He closed the tablet and looked up at Tess.

"Not implying anything. But it does seem we got plenty of motives to go around, and I haven't even talked to the nephew and his wife yet."

"Well," said Tess cautiously, "Edwina was inclined to squabbling with the other seniors. Actually, she seemed to enjoy it. But the sources of contention were usually trivial, like the disagreement with Ross over the locker. None of those conflicts seems like a motive for murder."

Butts picked up a pen and started a nervous tapping on the desk. "Maybe from your point of view, but somebody did murder her."

"Apparently that's true," Tess admitted.

Butts gazed at her for a long moment, a sizing-up expression on his face. "You've been around here long enough to notice a few things. You must have some opinions. Who do you think did it?"

Tess shook her head. "I really have no idea."

He looked as if he was disappointed in her. "Uh-huh. Well, as long as you're here and already got your nose in the situation, you might as well be of some use to me."

Tess let that pass without comment.

Butts hesitated, then said, "I'm gonna tell you something in confidence, provided you'll agree to cooperate with me. I need somebody on the inside who knows what's been going on with these people — or can find out without raising suspicion."

"Uh —" Tess wasn't sure whether to be flattered or offended. On previous occasions, Butts had told her to stay away from police business. She had helped Andy Neill clear up a murder investigation late last year, while Butts was out of town. Maybe Andy had told the Chief of the part she'd played. Of course, she wasn't enough of a fool to think that Butts actually liked her, but that wouldn't prevent his using her if he could. "I'll help if I can," she finally said.

He nodded solemnly, as if a pact had been signed. "The medical examiner said Miz Riley had a bunch of little puncture wounds on the pads of her fingers. He couldn't say how they got there, but it's possible the poison entered her body through those wounds. Weird, huh?"

"Not at all. She got those from quilting. Edwina didn't wear a thimble, so she was always pricking her fingers with her needles."

"Quilting?" Reflectively he looked down at his blunt hands, which were clasped together on the desk. When he looked up, his eyes flickered. "And everybody knew that Miz Riley didn't use a thimble?"

"Yes, all the quilters anyway. Actually, I'd say everybody here knew because I've heard Edwina complaining about stabbing herself with her needle several times after the quilting circle broke up."

"I'll start with the quilters."

Tess gave the names of the members of the quilting circle, and Butts wrote them down.

After a moment, he said, "So in all probability she touched something with the poison in it — or on it."

"That poison — I've forgotten what you called it . . ."

"Ricin," Butts said.

"Yes. Aside from the fact that whoever did this would have to have heard about it in the first place, how difficult would it be to get hold of some?"

"The M.E. says this ricin, which is one of the most poisonous substances known to man, can be purchased at pharmaceutical houses. He says an altered form of it is sometimes used to induce labor in pregnant women."

"But we don't have any pregnant women around here or any pharmaceutical houses in Victoria Springs. The killer could have gone to a large city to buy it, but wouldn't that require an ID? Wouldn't the buyer have to be a doctor or a hospital purchasing agent? I mean, surely they don't just hand poisons over to anybody who asks."

"That's what the M.E. said, so he thinks the killer cooked up his own poison."

"Good grief," Tess exclaimed. "That's hardly possible. Wouldn't that require a laboratory? Besides, none of these people has a pharmaceutical background that I know of. I doubt any of them has ever heard of ricin before today. I certainly haven't."

"You wouldn't need a laboratory or any special background. And by the way, everybody's heard of this poison — or rather the plant that contains it. Castor beans."

Tess gaped at him. "Castor beans! Why, I've seen them several places around town, in alleys mostly."

He nodded in agreement.

"In fact, Edwina has — had some in her front yard."

"Really?" He opened his tablet and made another note. Then, "The doc says the poisonous part's inside the bean. The crust is real hard, so you could swallow some beans whole and they probably wouldn't hurt you. According to the doc, you'd have to crush some of the beans, simmer them in a little water, remove the pulp, and boil the liquid down until you had enough poison concentrated in a drop or two to kill somebody — especially somebody who's old and physically not as able to fight the poison as a healthy younger person would be. The killer could have put it on almost anything that he knew Miz Riley would pick up. With all those breaks in the skin of her fingers" — he sucked in air and made a sound like somebody drawing the last drop of a soft drink through a straw — "it'd go straight to her bloodstream."

A memory flashed into Tess's mind. Edwina going through her sewing box the day before yesterday, after all the other quilters except Tess had left the room. She'd said something about her needles being discolored and dull and that she needed to get some new ones.

"Chief, it's possible the killer soaked Edwina's quilting needles in the poison." Tess went on to tell him what she'd remembered.

Butts's eyes widened and he lumbered up from behind the desk. "Where are those needles? At her house?"

"No, they're right here," Tess said, "in the sewing box in her locker — or the box was there the last time I noticed."

"Show me," Butts ordered and threw his arm out to indicate that she should precede him from the office.

The sewing box sat in the first cubbyhole in the bottom row, the space Ross and Edwina had wrangled over. The mystery novel Edwina had checked out from the local library lay on top of it.

"There it is," Tess said.

"These things don't even have doors," Butts barked. "That box was just sitting there for anybody to get into. Don't touch it. Can you get me a couple of plastic bags or paper sacks?"

Tess went to the kitchen and told Jenny what Butts needed. Jenny was plainly curious, but she asked no questions, and Tess did not volunteer anything. When she handed the plastic bags to Butts, he stuck his hands inside them and using them as mitts, lifted out the sewing box. Raising the lid, he peered inside.

Standing next to him, Tess scanned the contents of the box. There were several large spools of quilting thread in various colors and small plastic containers of straight pins and safety pins. Several needles lay loose at the bottom of the box, and they were oddly discolored. Tess had never seen quilting needles turn that dull, brownish color from ordinary use. A chill ran up her spine.

"Those needles don't look right," Butts observed.

"No, they don't."

"What do you want to bet they've been poisoned?"

Tess shook her head.

"I'll just take this whole basket with me," Butts said. "The lab can examine the other stuff along with the needles." He whipped out his ballpoint pen and used it to stir through the contents of the box. "It's all just sewing stuff," he said finally, "except for the ring."

"Edwina didn't wear jewelry," Tess said, bending closer to look into the box again.

"Then what's this doing in here?" With the pen, Butts touched a gaudy-looking costume ring with a green glass stone.

"That belongs to —" Tess halted and drew in a sharp breath.

"Who?" Butts demanded.

It was too late for Tess to call back the words now. Anyway, it would come out sooner or later. "It looks like a ring that Mercy Bates wore recently. She bought it at a garage sale. Maybe," Tess added hastily, "well, maybe

Edwina borrowed it."

"I thought you said Miz Riley never wore jewelry."

"That's true. But that ring was loose on Mercy's finger. It could have fallen off and Edwina could have picked it up. I don't want to speak ill of the dead, but it would have been just like Edwina to hide Mercy's ring to torment her."

Butts gave her a slit-eyed look. "Yeah, and if we find poison on Miz Riley's needles, the ring could've fallen off Mercy Bates's finger when she was poisoning them."

Tess nodded glumly. As reluctant as she was to think that Mercy had killed Edwina, she had to admit the possibility. When Mercy had phoned Tess at home, she'd been in such despair, and Tess had had the fleeting thought that Mercy, in that state of mind, might do almost anything to get Edwina out of her life for good. *I'm not going to let her hurt me anymore,* Mercy had said. *I'm going to put a stop to it once and for all.*

"Is Miz Bates still here?" Butts asked.

"If she's not, she'll be in her apartment out back," Tess told him. "Let me look around." Tess hoped to find Mercy and warn her before she faced the Chief.

Unfortunately, she had to return a few minutes later with the news that Mercy was not in the center. "Her apartment's number 2. You can go out the back door and around to get there. Shall I come with you?"

"You stay here," Butts snapped, conveniently forgetting his request that she cooperate in the investigation. What he had meant, of course, was that Tess should function as his spy inside the center and that he'd use her in any other ways he could think of, but she needn't expect him to reciprocate.

Butts stomped off, holding the sewing basket in front of him.

12

About fifteen minutes later, Tess saw Butts, through a rec room window, getting into his car. As soon as he'd driven out of sight, she put on her coat, let herself out, and walked back to Mercy's apartment. It was warmer today than the past few days, but a brisk wind nipped Tess's ears.

When Mercy opened the door, her eyes were red and her face was streaked with smeared mascara. "Oh, Tess!" she cried, "Have you heard? Chief Butts found my ring in Edwina's sewing box. He — he ac-accused me of killing her! He said I lost my ring when I was pu-putting poison on Edwina's sewing supplies."

"Calm down, Mercy," Tess said. "Butts will accuse us all of the murder before he's through. It's his way."

Fresh tears streamed down Mercy's sagging cheeks. "No, Tess, I think he really believes I did it." She wiped her eyes with the back of her hand. "I'm a nervous wreck! Oh — oh, I'm sorry. I'm keeping you standing there in the cold. Would you like to come in?"

"Thank you." Tess entered a living-room-kitchen area. It was small but tidy. Mercy's furniture was worn, but she had brightened the room with a wine-and-green floral print fabric for sofa throw pillows and the valance at the window.

Tess took off her coat and draped it across the back of a maple rocker, where she then sat down.

Mercy slumped on the sofa, clutching a flowered pillow to her breast. "Are they going to arrest me, Tess?" Her voice wobbled.

"No. Your ring being in Edwina's sewing box doesn't prove anything." Mercy was looking at her intently, as if she desperately wanted to believe Tess's words. "Do you have any idea how your ring ended up with Edwina's quilting supplies?"

Mercy shook her head hard several times. "No! I didn't put it there, Tess. I never even touched Edwina's sewing box, I swear. You know how she was. I never touched anything of Edwina's because she was so crabby about her things."

"When was the last time you remember seeing the ring?"

Mercy took another swipe at her eyes and seemed to be thinking it over. Finally she said, "I think I was wearing it the day Wally came to the book discussion."

Tess nodded, remembering that she'd noticed the ring on Mercy's finger that day, the day before Edwina was poisoned, the day before Edwina noticed that her needles were discolored.

Mercy squeezed her eyes closed for a long moment. "That's the last time I remember."

"Do you recall taking it off when you came back to your apartment that day?"

Mercy pondered and shook her head. "I just don't have any memory of the ring after Wally was here. It was loose and almost came off once or twice during the book discussion. I probably still had it on at lunch that day, but I honestly don't remember that specifically."

"I noticed that it was loose, too," Tess said. "You could have lost it anywhere in the center. Are you sure you don't remember taking it off that evening?"

"I'm sorry, Tess, but I simply have no recollection of the ring after the book discussion. Chief Butts badgered me and badgered me, trying to make me remember more, but I couldn't." Reaching for a tissue from the box on the side table next to the sofa, Mercy blew her nose, then took a fresh tissue to wipe her eyes. She stared at the tissue. "Oh, Lord, I'm wiping mascara everywhere. Excuse me for a minute, Tess."

While Mercy was gone, Tess thought back to the day before Edwina died, the day she'd noticed the ring on Mercy's finger. Try as she might, she could not remember seeing it after the book discussion. Sometime after that, but probably the same day, Mercy had lost the ring — if Mercy was being truthful. Then one of two things had happened. Either Edwina found the ring and hid it in her sewing box. Or the killer found it and left it in Edwina's sewing box to throw suspicion on Mercy when he or she dipped the needles in the homemade poison. If that's what happened, Tess wondered if the killer had wanted to lead the police to Mercy in particular. Or had the ring given him or her the idea? In which case, any scapegoat would have served. Because of the ring, it just happened to be Mercy.

The final possibility, as Chief Butts had pointed out, was that the ring had slipped off Mercy's finger when she poisoned the needles, a scenario that Tess still had trouble crediting. Yet Mercy had been at the end of her rope with Edwina.

When Mercy returned, her face was scrubbed clean. Tess had never seen Mercy without her makeup before. Uncovered, the lines in her pale face were even more prominent, and her sparse eyebrows were shot with gray, which made them fade into the background of her face, as if she had no eyebrows at all. Mercy looked more vulnerable somehow without her paint and powder.

She sat on the sofa and clutched the throw pillow again.

"Mercy, you were extremely upset when you called me the other night. I didn't go into detail about that conversation with Chief Butts, but if he pins me down, wants to know what you said, I'll have to tell him."

She looked at Tess, her bottom lip trembling. She caught it between her teeth. "You sound like you think I killed Edwina." She reached for a fresh tissue and dabbed at her eyes.

"No, I don't. I'm trying to look at it from Butts's point of view. From what I've heard, you and Edwina go back a long way, to your school days. Was that in Victoria Springs?"

She shook her head. "A little town about fifty miles from here. You probably wouldn't even call it a town now. It's dwindled to a few houses and a convenience store, but when I was in school there, we had fifty-three in our graduating class."

"You and Edwina were in the same class?"

"Yes, and Gerald."

"Your late husband?"

She nodded and bit her lip. "And Edwina's."

Tess stared at her, not sure she understood. "Are you saying that Gerald was once married to Edwina?"

A tear leaked out and trickled down Mercy's cheek. She wiped it away. "He married her first. She — she tricked him into it. She was jealous."

"Jealous? Of you?"

"Of what Gerald and I had together. We were high school sweethearts, and we planned to marry soon after graduation. Edwina and I were best friends all through high school. She wasn't so mean then, or I was too dumb to realize it. She said things — about other people, you know — but I thought she was being funny. Edwina had a reputation then of being a card. Our senior year, when I started spending so much time with Gerald, she couldn't stand it. She was envious or she felt left out or something. We stayed friends, but we didn't do everything together as we had before."

"Because you were with Gerald."

Agitatedly Mercy wadded the tissue in her hand. "Edwina and I had had our falling-outs, like all kids do, and I knew she could be vindictive. But she got worse as she got older. Even back then, I was usually the one who apologized when we made up, because she wouldn't, but I never thought she'd do what she did."

"Which was?"

Mercy held the pillow tighter and looked down at her lap. "She — she got her dad's old car one night after Gerald had taken me home, and went by his house and talked him into going for a ride with her. She'd brought along a dozen or so cans of her dad's beer. Gerald wasn't used to drinking, you see." She expelled a heavy sigh. "To make a long story short, she got Gerald drunk and then she seduced him." Tess must have looked skeptical, for she added, "Oh, I know it wasn't all Edwina's fault. Gerald didn't have to get drunk or have sex with her. He didn't have to get in the car with her in the first place. But he did, and Edwina couldn't wait to get to school the next day and tell me about Gerald's betrayal."

Knowing Edwina, Tess could easily believe what Mercy was saying.

Mercy went on, "That's when I first knew how truly mean she could be. She said Gerald told her he didn't really want to marry me but he didn't know how to get out of it. Gerald swore he never said anything of the kind, and I believed him. But that didn't make me feel a whole lot better. Naturally I was crushed that he'd slept with her." Her mouth twisted. "I was saving myself for marriage. I always assumed Edwina was, too. In those days, if a girl went all the way, she didn't tell."

She glanced away toward the window, but Tess didn't think she was really seeing it. She was seeing fifty-year-old pictures in her mind. "Gerald begged me to forgive him and take him back," she said at last, "and finally I did."

Tess was beginning to understand what happened next. "Let me guess. Edwina turned up pregnant?"

Mercy returned her look to Tess's face. Long-buried hatred glimmered in her naked eyes. "That's what she said, Tess, but I'll always believe it was a lie. Gerald was with her only that one time. But he was incredibly naive. We both were. And when Edwina called him that summer after our graduation and told him she was pregnant and it was his baby because she hadn't been with anybody else, he — well, he thought he had to marry her. It was a small town. Everybody knew everybody else's business. And back then, when a boy got a girl pregnant, he was expected to marry her. I was just getting to the point where I didn't think about what Gerald had done every time we were together. I'd forgiven him, but I had a hard time forgetting. Then Edwina called him. She never loved him, of course. I'm not sure now that Edwina was even capable of real love. She just wanted to punish me for being happy and planning a life with Gerald. I'm convinced that if Gerald and I hadn't gotten back together, Edwina would never have made that call."

"So they married."

"Ye—es," she said, her voice breaking on a sob. After a moment, when she'd composed herself again, she continued, "They moved to Victoria Springs and with the help of Gerald's parents bought a little house — the house where Edwina lived for the rest of her life. Two months after the wedding, Edwina told Gerald that she'd miscarried. He believed her at first, even though she had never seen a doctor. He was so gullible. But he'd never dealt with anyone as devious as Edwina. As I said, I never believed she was pregnant in the first place."

Only now was Tess starting to grasp the depths of Edwina's cruelty.

"The marriage fell apart soon after that,"

Mercy murmured. "Gerald left her with the house and what little savings they had, and Edwina filed for a divorce. The day the divorce was final, Gerald was on my doorstep, begging my forgiveness again."

"It must have been much harder the second time."

Mercy nodded. "At first I didn't think I could do it. It took a lot longer for me to trust him, but eventually we started dating again and eighteen months after the divorce, we were married. He was a good husband, Tess. I never for a minute regretted marrying him." Mercy sighed. "Unfortunately we had to live in Victoria Springs because Gerald had a good job and he thought he couldn't afford to give it up. For years, Edwina and I didn't even speak when we saw each other on the street. But after Gerald's death, when I moved here to the center, we saw each other almost every day of the week. It seemed pointless to hold onto a grudge after all that time. Actually, I felt sorry for Edwina. She never married again, had no real friends. I — I tried to be civil to her, when she'd let me."

Mercy may not have wanted to hold a fifty-year-old grudge, but Tess was remembering the cruel little jibes Edwina had directed at Mercy. Hard as it was for Tess to understand, Edwina, after all those years, still resented Mercy's happy marriage.

"I know now it was a mistake, asking Wally to

come to the center. When Edwina saw us together, she was determined to destroy our relationship — just like she almost destroyed what I had with Gerald."

Poor Mercy, Tess mused. She had seen the past with Gerald happening all over again with Wally. Enough to make anyone wish Edwina dead, if not actually carry out the murder. "No wonder you were so upset," Tess murmured. "Did you tell Chief Butts that Gerald and Edwina were once married?"

"Uh-huh. He scared me so bad I blabbed everything I knew."

"It's best that you did," Tess said. "If you hadn't and he'd found out later you'd kept something from him, that would have been worse for you."

"It seems that all my life, whenever something bad happened, it could be traced back to Edwina. Why did she have to be so hurtful, Tess?"

"I don't think Edwina liked herself or her life, though I doubt she would ever have admitted it. So she took it out on whoever was handy, especially people who seemed to be content with their lot."

Mercy frowned. "It was as if she had a big secret that nobody else knew. Something she enjoyed holding close, keeping hidden. Sometimes I had the feeling she was laughing at people because she knew something they didn't. Do you understand what I mean?"

"Yes," Tess mused. "Maybe it wasn't one big secret but a lot of little ones. Like the fact that she knew private things about Gerald because she'd been married to him."

Mercy nodded. "And she might broadcast what she knew all over town if I made her too mad. It seems silly now, the way I let her get under my skin. I knew Gerald better than anybody and Edwina couldn't have known anything scandalous about him." Her brow furrowed. "I guess I was afraid she'd make something up."

"People who knew Edwina and Gerald probably wouldn't have believed her."

"I don't know, Tess. Sometimes people want to believe the worst of other people."

"Some people, maybe. But Gerald's been gone for several years. Nothing Edwina said could have mattered much."

"I suppose so," Mercy said. She rested her chin on the edge of the throw pillow. After a thoughtful moment, her eyes flew to Tess. "And you're sure Chief Butts can't arrest me because he found my ring in Edwina's sewing box?"

"They haven't even tested the contents of the box yet, Mercy. And even if they find the poison, I'm sure they'd have to have more than the ring," Tess assured her. "Anybody could have put it there."

She mulled that over. "To hurt me, you mean?"

"Not necessarily. But to divert suspicion from themselves."

Mercy frowned. "Why does Chief Butts think the poison is in Edwina's sewing box?"

Tess realized she'd probably already said too much. "I don't know, Mercy, but try not to worry about it."

Somewhat cheered by Tess's words, Mercy looked encouraged. "Between you and me, Tess, I'm glad she's gone."

A view that would be shared by several other people, Tess thought, but she hoped Mercy wouldn't say that where anyone else could hear her.

13

Upon reaching the McBrooms' apartment on her way back to the center, Tess saw Anita sitting in a chair by the window, reading. Remembering that Butts wanted her to find out what had destroyed the friendship between the McBrooms and Edwina, Tess tapped on the door.

Looking up, Anita smiled and waved, then got up to open the door. "Hi, Tess. What're you up to?"

"I've been with Mercy. She's not taking this very well." Tess decided not to mention the ring. Eventually everybody would hear about it, but not from her.

"Come on in," Anita invited. "Albert's gone for a walk. How about a cup of tea?"

"Tea would be nice. Thanks."

After removing her coat, Tess sat at the small table by a side window while Anita prepared their drinks.

"Frankly, I can't imagine why Mercy's upset," Anita said as she placed tea bags in two cups. "The way Edwina tormented her — well, you'd think Mercy would be glad to have it ended."

"She and Edwina go back a long way."

"Edwina wasn't her friend. Edwina wasn't anybody's friend. She only pretended to be when it served her purpose."

Tess wondered if that's what had happened to the McBrooms. Had Edwina pretended to be their friend, then turned on them? But how? What could she have done?

"Mercy and Edwina grew up together," Tess said, noting how Anita's mouth thinned with distaste as she spoke. "And you know Mercy, she's tender-hearted."

Anita poured hot water into the cups and brought them to the table. "It doesn't pay to be tender-hearted with people like Edwina."

No grief here, Tess thought, *not even a smidgen of compassion for the late Edwina.*

Before Tess could frame a response, Anita asked, "What do you want in your tea?"

"Nothing, thanks."

Anita sat down, lifted her cup in both hands. Staring beyond Tess, she blew on the hot tea to cool it.

Tess tried to think how best to put her question, but there seemed to be no subtle way to say it. "Anita, Jenny told me that when you and Albert first moved to Victoria Springs, Edwina was a close friend."

Anita gazed at her, her expression revealing nothing. "As I said, it doesn't pay to get close to Edwina. I found that out. She pretends to confide in you, then when you do the same . . ." Her voice trailed off and she avoided eye contact with Tess by looking out the window again.

It sounded as if Anita had told Edwina something that Edwina tried to use against her. "What happened to break up the friendship?"

Anita set her cup down. Staring at her tea, she said, "It wasn't any single thing, Tess, just a lot of little things. For one, she took advantage of Albert, always calling him to fix something in her house. The first couple of times, he didn't mind, but she wouldn't stop."

"Why didn't he refuse?" Tess asked.

Anita looked up, her eyes suddenly blazing, but instead of answering Tess's question, she said, "She got mad when his back started bothering him and he couldn't provide free labor for her anymore. She actually accused him of faking it. After his surgery, she expected him to go back to doing her repairs."

But why hadn't Albert ignored Edwina? He hadn't owed her anything — or had he?

Anita wrapped her fingers around her cup. The knuckles turned white. Tess feared her grip was hard enough to shatter the china. It was expensive-looking china, too. A constant reminder of better times in the McBrooms' marriage?

Anita went on, "You've seen how much Albert's back still bothers him, Tess. It's almost as bad as it was before the surgery. I couldn't believe Edwina meant to keep badgering him. But that woman knew no shame. She was relentless. She even got poor Albert to give back that locker in the bottom row."

"I don't understand why Albert did that, Anita."

She merely shook her head and said, "Let's talk about something else, Tess. This is too depressing."

Edwina wouldn't badger Albert anymore, Tess thought, and again Albert's words came back to her: *How long would they have to put up with Edwina?* Anita had asked. Albert's answer: *Till we're dead, or she is.* Earlier he had said, *Whatever Edwina wants, Edwina gets. And don't forget whose fault that is.* Had he meant that it was Anita's fault?

That was another indication that Anita had told Edwina something in confidence, something Edwina had turned against her. But Tess couldn't think of any way to ask Anita point-blank without revealing that she'd eavesdropped on the McBrooms' private conversation. Besides, it was becoming quite clear that Anita wasn't going to tell her.

Perhaps it was only people with nothing to hide who told everything they knew in a murder investigation. If that was true, then Mercy was not the killer. And perhaps Anita or Albert was. From the conversation she'd overheard, Tess was sure that the McBrooms had wanted Edwina to leave them alone but didn't think she would. Because, Tess now thought, of something Anita had done to Edwina or something she had confided to her. Whatever that was, Edwina had been using it to blackmail Albert into doing her bidding.

Subtly Tess tried again to find out more but got nowhere. And Anita began making noises about having things to do. Finally Tess took the hint, thanked Anita for the tea, and left. Walking back to the center, she now thought she knew at least that Edwina had used blackmail to get her way. And if she'd blackmailed the McBrooms, she could have done it to others.

Tess found Jenny in her office entering figures from several sheets of paper into a laptop computer. Jenny smiled when she saw Tess. "This is the part I hate about running the center," she said. "If you get money from the government, you have to fill out endless reports." She logged off and folded the computer screen down over the keys.

"Don't let me interrupt you."

"Oh, I can fiddle with the figures anytime." She stuck the papers into a manila envelope, then bent to slide out a shallow tray from beneath the desk. The tray could not be seen when it was pushed all the way in unless you lay on the floor. Jenny put the manila envelope into the tray and closed it. "My secret hiding place," she explained as she straightened up. "I bought this desk used and I'd had it for months before I discovered that drawer. The former owner must have installed it, because I'm sure it wasn't part of the original desk."

"I'd never have guessed it was there," Tess said.

"Nobody knows about it but me — and now you. You won't tell anybody, will you?"

"My lips are sealed," Tess assured her.

Jenny sighed. "I take out my records and the computer every week and mess around with the figures. Problem is, no matter how much I juggle, I still can't come up with quite enough money to pay cash for the kitchen remodeling. We've about finished paying off the property and had hoped we wouldn't have to take out another loan for the kitchen."

Having done a complete remodeling of Iris House before she opened her bed and breakfast, Tess knew how expensive construction projects were and could sympathize. "Willis's doing the work will help a lot."

"Oh, yes. Otherwise, we couldn't do it at all this year."

Tess told Jenny about her conversation with Anita, adding, "She wouldn't tell me what destroyed her friendship with Edwina, but whatever it was, she's still gets angry thinking about it."

Jenny frowned thoughtfully. "I know. I tried to find out a couple of times, but the McBrooms would only say that Edwina wasn't the person they'd thought she was. I even asked Edwina once, and she just gave me a smug little smile."

Tess had seen Edwina smile that way several times when she was having a disagreement with another person at the center. Mercy was right. It was as if Edwina knew secrets about everybody that they didn't want revealed, but now Edwina was gone and supposedly the secrets were safe.

Jenny was studying Tess's face. "What's wrong, Tess? You can't think the McBrooms killed her."

"I don't know," Tess said honestly. "What do you know about them?"

"Very little, really. Albert was a middle-school principal in Texas, a little town called Verily or Verity — no, Vanity. That's it, Vanity, Texas. I believe Anita was a secretary in the superintendent's office. When they retired, they moved to Victoria Springs."

"Why here?"

"I wondered that myself. I thought at first that they must have ties here, but I asked Anita once and she said, no, they wanted a smallish town with decent low-income housing. I gather their retirement income isn't much."

"How long have they lived here?"

"Oh, they were among our very first tenants, after we got the apartments ready. That was almost ten years ago."

Tess did a quick calculation. "They must

have been in their fifties when they retired."

"I think so, yes."

"But why would they retire early, knowing they'd have to cut living expenses to the bone?"

Jenny shrugged. "You hear horror stories about schools these days. Maybe the discipline problem got to be too much for Albert, with his physical ailments."

"Maybe," Tess said. "Anyway, the McBrooms certainly aren't the only ones who are glad to see Edwina gone."

Jenny closed the manila folder that lay open on her desk and tucked it into a desk drawer. "Sad but true. Now that we've all gotten over the initial shock of Edwina's death, I've noticed that the other seniors seem more relaxed than before. Not as wary of each other as they were when Edwina was part of the mix."

Tess said, "I have to admit the atmosphere around here will be more pleasant without her." She frowned. "How's that for an epitaph?"

Jenny nodded glumly. "Sad, isn't it? Frankly, I thought once or twice about asking Edwina not to come back to the center. But then she'd say something about how important the center was to her, and I just couldn't." A smile flickered on her face. "I think she suspected what I wanted to say once, because she leaned over and whispered to me that she'd left me a little something in her will. It was like a bribe." Jenny chuckled. "Do you suppose she left me some of her old magazines?"

Tess laughed. "Don't knock it. From what I've seen, those magazines could go back thirty or forty years, even longer. A few of them could actually be valuable."

Jenny shuddered. "I'm not sure it would be worth digging through all that accumulation to find the valuable ones. The worth of the whole lot of them couldn't amount to more than a few hundred dollars. Throw in the furniture, and the lot would still not be valued at much more."

Jenny's words had reminded Tess of something she'd forgotten. "You said Edwina told you she'd left you a little something in her will. You know, she said the same thing to me — those exact words — the last day I drove her to the center before her nephew got here. It was kind of a throwaway remark in the middle of something else she was saying, and I didn't put any stock in it. I'd forgotten all about it until just now."

Jenny shook her head. "She must have thought you were getting tired of taxiing her to and from the center and wanted to give you an incentive. I'll bet she told that to anybody she needed to stay on the good side of."

Remembering the conversation between Skip and Milly she'd overheard, Tess said, "I think she promised her nephew something in her will, too. I suppose she was lonely and used that to get Skip and Milly to come visit her."

"Poor thing. She barely managed to get by on her social security. Did she think people didn't know that? It's sad, really." Jenny pursed her lips. "The funeral's tomorrow morning at the funeral home chapel. I don't think any of the seniors are going. I will, I guess. I really feel I should. I don't expect anybody else to be there except the nephew and his wife. Maybe Willis, if I can talk him into it."

"I'll stay here to keep an eye on things for you."

"Oh, good. Thank you, Tess."

Upon leaving the center, Tess decided to drop by the Queen Street Book Shop for a chat with her cousin. Cinny, of course, had heard about the medical examiner's autopsy findings. It was difficult to keep anything secret in Victoria Springs.

When they were settled with cups of fresh coffee on a settee in the bookshop, Tess filled Cinny in on what she knew about the investigation, omitting her and Butts's suspicion that Edwina's quilting needles had carried the poison that killed her. If the lab bore out their suspicion, the news would make its way along the grapevine soon enough.

"I can't believe Edwina was once married to Gerald Bates," Cinny exclaimed when Tess finished.

"It boggles the mind," Tess agreed. "I never knew Gerald, of course, but two more dissimilar women than Edwina and Mercy I can't imagine."

"You say Butts took Edwina's sewing box? Does he think Edwina stole Mercy's ring, the one he found in Edwina's box?"

"I'm not sure what he thinks. He said something about checking the sewing box for fingerprints."

"It doesn't look too good for Mercy, does it?"

"She's frightened out of her wits of being arrested," Tess said. "I tried to reassure her, but I'm not sure it helped much."

"When will he know about the fingerprints?"

Tess shrugged. "Maybe by tomorrow. Regardless of what they find, unless the murderer is caught soon, Mercy is going to worry herself sick."

"My money's on Ross Dellin," Cinny confided. "That man is an explosion waiting to happen. And Edwina did accuse him of poisoning her."

Tess sighed, wondering how Cinny had come by that bit of information. Through Cody Yount, probably. Cinny had been dating the young attorney for nine months now, a record for Cinny. Tess thought the relationship must be getting serious. As a defense attorney, Cody knew everybody on the police force. One of the officers must have told him about Edwina's dying accusation, and Cody had passed it on to Cinny. "Edwina made a practice of accusing Ross of first one thing and then another. The whole time I've been volunteering at the center, they've had a running battle going."

"Only this time, Edwina died — of poison."

"True. But I'd still like to know what happened between Edwina and the McBrooms."

Cinny looked contemplative, then she got a calculating gleam in her eyes. "You said Albert took early retirement from the middle school in Vanity, Texas." She jumped up and carried her empty coffee cup to the customer counter. "Let's play detective, Tess," she said, sliding onto a stool and pushing the phone toward Tess.

Not a single customer had come into the bookshop since Tess's arrival. Business was virtually nonexistent, and Cinny was bored.

Tess joined her at the counter. "I'm not sure we should do anything without Chief Butts's approval, Cinny."

Cinny frowned at her. "Since when did that bother you? You've carried out your own little investigations before now."

"This is different."

"I don't see how."

Frankly, Tess couldn't quite verbalize her vague misgivings. "What did you have in mind?"

"Calling the superintendent's office in Vanity, Texas. Maybe the McBrooms didn't leave there voluntarily."

Tess's doubts were dissipated. Whoever answered the phone in the superintendent's office probably wouldn't reveal anything to a strange woman calling long distance. But she'd have to prove it to Cinny. She picked up the telephone receiver, got the number from information, and dialed.

A woman answered in Vanity, and Tess said, "Vanessa Freely in Victoria Springs, Missouri, here." Cinny gave her a thumbs up sign. "As president of our local school board," Tess went on, "I'm checking references on several people who've applied to be substitute teachers." She added in a confidential tone, "I'm sure you know how difficult it is to find enough qualified substitutes."

"Yes, indeed," the woman said. "It's virtually impossible."

"That's so true," Tess said. "All the same, we can't be too careful in checking out applicants. Which brings me to my business with you. One of our applicants gave this number as a reference. His name is Albert McBroom. According to his application, he worked as a middle-school principal in your system."

"McBroom, you say?" The woman's tone had turned wary. "I'm afraid I can't help you. Would you like to speak to Ms. Vandever, the superintendent?"

"Yes, please."

Tess covered the mouthpiece and whispered to Cinny, "She got cautious all of a sudden. She's putting me through to the superintendent."

At the other end of the line, a businesslike

voice said, "This is the superintendent."

Uncovering the mouthpiece, Tess said, "Hello. Thank you for taking my call, Ms. Vandever. I'm checking references on Albert McBroom."

"I'm not sure I can give you that information. The privacy laws, you know."

"I understand perfectly, Ms. Vandever. I appreciate your dilemma, but I'm sure you appreciate my position, as well. Children are, after all, our first consideration, as I'm sure you will agree."

"I can't dispute that."

"Why don't I ask a few questions. You can answer or not, as you wish. All right?"

"Very well."

Amazed that she'd gotten that far, Tess grabbed a piece of paper and, with pen poised, said, "First, let's clear up the question of Mr. McBroom's employment. Was he, in fact, a middle-school principal in your system?"

"I'll have to check my files."

Tess covered the mouthpiece and whispered to Cinny, "She's gone to check her files. I think she's stalling for time."

When the superintendent came back, she said, "Yes, Albert McBroom was a school principal here."

Cinny grabbed Tess's pen and scribbled on the paper. Tess scanned Cinny's note hurriedly before asking, "How long was Mr. McBroom employed there?"

"Twelve years."

Tess wrote "12" beside Cinny's note. "And would you say he was a good employee?"

"He was punctual, didn't have excessive absences. He was named teacher of the year when he was still in the classroom."

"That would be before he was named principal?" Tess asked.

"That's correct."

"What about his retirement? Was it voluntary?"

After a long pause, the superintendent said, "Technically."

Technically? Tess thought. That could mean he was strongly urged to retire by the school board, maybe even given an ultimatum: retire or be fired.

"All things considered," Tess said, "this applicant seems promising. Sounds like you would hire him as a substitute yourself, if he were applying there."

There was a long pause on the other end of the line. Then, "I wouldn't put it that way."

"Oh? How would you put it then?" Tess asked.

"Let's just say I wouldn't want to be responsible for placing Mr. McBroom in a position where he has access to minors. That's all I'm prepared to say on the subject. I have an appointment. Good-bye."

Tess heard a dial tone. She hung up and repeated to Cinny what the superintendent had said.

Cinny's mouth dropped open. "She wouldn't give him access to minors? She actually said that?"

Tess nodded. "Her exact words."

"What else?"

"That's all. Obviously I'm to draw my own conclusions."

"I can't believe she gave you that much."

"Neither can I."

"Darn, you're good, Tess," Cinny said admiringly.

Tess grinned. "I am, aren't I?" She sobered. "Do you think I can get in trouble for impersonating a school board president?"

"Don't worry about it. She's not going to check up on you. She's probably already regretting that she said as much as she did. She won't want to get in any deeper."

Tess nodded. Cinny was probably right. "Even if she does check, they can't trace the call back to me — I don't think." She was silent for a moment, mulling over the superintendent's warning. "She wouldn't give Albert access to minors. What does that mean?"

"Maybe he had a fling with one of his students."

"He was a middle-school principal. That's sixth through eighth grade usually. Roughly, ages eleven through thirteen. Kind of young."

"Maybe he likes 'em young. It happens, Tess."

Propping her elbows on the counter, Tess put

her head in her hands. "God, I hope not. But if that's what Edwina found out, it sure would make good blackmail material."

"How can we get the details without subjecting ourselves to a lawsuit?" Cinny wondered.

Maybe she could bluff the truth out of Anita McBroom, Tess thought. To her surprise, bluffing had just worked with the school superintendent in Vanity. But she'd first have to convince Anita that she already knew why Albert was forced to retire and merely wanted to warn Anita that it might become public knowledge.

"I know," Cinny said suddenly. "We'll ask Cody."

"Cinny, I don't think Cody will want to get involved in this."

"He won't get involved. We'll just ask him a few questions off the record. We're having dinner at Hudson's tonight. Could you and Luke join us?"

Cinny would probably ask Cody, whether Tess was present or not. "I think so. We're going out anyway."

"Call him," Cinny urged.

Tess reached for the phone. "I won't tell him we want to talk about the murder investigation. Luke thinks I should stay out of it."

Cinny rolled her eyes. "So what else is new? He's doing the macho thing, protecting his woman. It's kind of cute, actually."

14

Hudson's was a popular Victoria Springs restaurant specializing in grilled steaks and fresh seafood, which was flown into Springfield daily, where it was picked up by a Hudson employee. During the tourist season, getting in without a long wait, even if you had a reservation, was virtually impossible. Tess tried to avoid the restaurant during that time. But at seven o'clock on a mid-February evening, the place was only half-full.

Tess and Luke had met Cinny and Cody at the restaurant, and they had been seated immediately at a table in one of the small, private alcoves running along two walls of the main dining area. In the alcoves, people could have a full view of the restaurant while carrying on private conversations.

Tess could tell by looking at Cinny that she was still fired up about their "investigation." As soon as they'd exchanged greetings and a few other casual preliminaries, Cinny launched into a detailed account of the hard feelings between Edwina Riley and the McBrooms and Tess's phone call to the school superintendent in Vanity, Texas.

When she finished, Luke gave Tess a slanted smile and said, "God help us, Cody. It runs in the family."

Tess made a stab at defending herself. "Actually, Chief Butts asked me to find out what I could about the people at the center."

Cody laughed. "Butts must be desperate."

Tess frowned at the uncomplimentary remark, but possibly Cody only meant that it was unprofessional of Butts to involve a civilian in a murder investigation.

Luke took Tess's hand. "I know you'll do what you want to do, sweetheart, so watch your back."

"What we were wondering, Cody," Cinny went on, "is how we can find out what really happened to Albert McBroom in Vanity, Texas, without subjecting ourselves to a lawsuit."

"This is a sticky situation, hon," Cody told her. "I can check and find out if McBroom was ever charged with a crime. If there was a trial, all those records are public. Criminals and public figures give up much of their right to privacy. But if he has no criminal record, you can't go around asking questions that can be interpreted as slander — not and hope to get away with it."

Luke listened intently and nodded throughout Cody's statement. Clearly he was hoping Tess was getting the message.

"Can you check that tomorrow?" Cinny asked.

"Sure." Cody looked at Luke and shrugged. "If you can't beat 'em, join 'em."

"Good," said Cinny. "Tess, I'll let you know as soon as I do."

Since they would accomplish nothing by discussing the situation further — except more cautionary warnings from Luke and Cody — Tess quickly changed the subject.

Though she hadn't previously gone to the center on weekends, Tess stayed there for an hour Saturday morning so that Jenny and Willis could attend Edwina's funeral. The place was as quiet as a tomb. The Bloom sisters, Mercy, and Don Bob had decided to go to the funeral after all. And none of the other regulars put in an appearance while Tess was there.

Saturday afternoon, Cinny phoned Tess at home. "Cody just called. Albert McBroom has no police record."

"I see." Tess didn't know whether to be glad — for the McBrooms — or disappointed because the search had provided no new information. "Looks like our luck ran out. So that's that, I guess."

"Surely we're not giving up that easily!"

"You heard Cody. If we keep poking around, we could get in big trouble."

"Oh, that." Cinny brushed it aside. "Cody's a lawyer. Lawyers see potential lawsuits everywhere. To hear them tell it, you can't step out of your house without getting sued."

"What you're suggesting is a little more than stepping out of the house," Tess asserted.

"I'm not suggesting anything in particular. We just have to think of a sneaky way to find out what Albert was up to in Texas."

"What, for instance?"

"I don't know yet, but it'll be simpler all around if we don't mention this to Cody and Luke."

On that point, Tess couldn't agree more. She'd fill Luke in afterward, if she learned anything new. "Let's both think about it," Tess said. "I'll get back to you if I come up with anything." Tess preferred following up on the McBrooms alone. She knew her cousin, and Cinny could get carried away, get too self-confident, talk too much, go too far. Especially when she was idle and bored.

Tess and Luke spent most of Sunday together, but she didn't mention the murder investigation. Nor did Luke, who donned a raincoat and galoshes against the chill February drizzle and spent part of the afternoon wandering around outside Iris House, snapping pictures with the camera he'd brought with him and writing things on a notepad.

When he came in for a cup of hot chocolate, Tess asked what he had been up to. He merely smiled mysteriously and said, "You'll know very soon, love."

Before Tess left for the center Monday morning, she received a startling phone call. The caller identified herself as Shelly Dawes, secretary to attorney James Fillbrook of Springfield, Missouri. "Is this the Tess Darcy who operates a bed and breakfast called Iris House?"

"Yes," said Tess, thinking that it was somebody wanting to make a reservation.

"I'm calling to request that you be present for the reading of the will of Edwina Riley. You are one of the beneficiaries."

Tess had to sit down. "What? But I thought . . ." She'd thought Edwina was lying when she said she'd left Tess "a little something" in her will, thought that Edwina had used the promise to insure that Tess would continue to chauffeur her around.

"Yes?" prompted the secretary.

"Never mind. When and where will the reading be?"

"Since most of the beneficiaries live in Victoria Springs, Mr. Fillbrook has arranged for a meeting room at Lake Country Savings and Loan. Do you know where that is?"

"On Hill Street across from City Hall."

"Can you be there at two tomorrow afternoon?"

"Yes."

"Good. Just say you're meeting Mr. Fillbrook, and they'll show you to the meeting room. Now, perhaps you can help me locate another heir. Steven Hector. We've tried reaching him at his home in Fort Worth, we've even left messages on the answering machine, but he hasn't gotten back to us."

Steven Hector? That had to be Skip. "I think you're referring to Edwina's nephew. I know him as Skip."

"That's right, Mr. Hector is Ms. Riley's nephew."

"He's here, staying in my bed and breakfast with his wife. I can transfer you to their room, if you'd like."

"I'd appreciate that."

Tess made the transfer and hung up. Then she sat for a moment, pondering the phone call. What on earth could Edwina have left her? Please, God, don't let it be some of her junk collection. Like Jenny, Tess didn't think rifling through it would be worth the effort.

But there was no point in speculating. She'd deal with whatever it was when she had to.

As soon as she reached the center, she found Jenny and told her about the phone call.

"I got a call from that attorney, too," Jenny said. "Willis answered the phone and took the message. I'm still in shock. I didn't believe Edwina when she said she was leaving me something. Willis said not to get my hopes up, that it's probably not much."

"I didn't believe Edwina, either, but what Willis says is true. It can't be much."

Jenny made a face. "Still, I feel guilty now for

the unkind thoughts I had about Edwina."

During lunch that afternoon at the center, Tess overheard Anita McBroom saying to her husband that she wanted to go to The Quilters Nook to pick up a new Sunbonnet Sue quilt-pattern book. Sunbonnet Sue quilts were Anita's specialty. Albert responded that his back was bothering him and he wasn't in a mood to stand around while she browsed through books and fabrics. Besides, he needed to take the car in for an oil change.

As soon as Albert was gone, Tess intercepted Anita. "I can take you to The Quilters Nook, Anita. I'd like to pick up a schedule of the classes they're offering this spring."

Anita was delighted. "Oh, thank you, Tess. I'll run and get my purse. Be right back."

The two women spent a pleasant half-hour at The Quilters Nook, fingering colorful fabrics and browsing through books and other supplies. Anita found the book she wanted and they left the shop.

As Tess backed out of the parking space, she said, "Anita, I've been trying to decide how to tell you something, and — well, there seems to be no gentle way, so I'll just come out with it."

Anita shot her a puzzled look. "What is it, Tess?"

"The investigation has turned up something I think you should know about before Chief Butts confronts Albert with it."

"Butts!" Anita blurted, the sudden anger in her tone taking Tess by surprise. "I knew that man was going to poke around in everybody's life like a — a vulture."

Tess was thankful that Anita had assumed it was Butts's investigation that Tess had referred to. "It seems that Albert was forced into early retirement in Texas over . . . er . . . inappropriate behavior with a minor." Tess stopped for a light and stole a quick glance at Anita, whose face had paled, though her eyes blazed.

"What in God's name has that got to do with Edwina's death?"

"I believe," Tess said carefully, accelerating again, "there is some indication that Edwina might have been blackmailing people, finding out things they didn't want known and using that to extort favors."

Anita fumed in silence for a moment. Then, "We should have told her to stay away from us at the beginning, but Albert thought if we humored her, she'd soon leave us alone. Hah!"

"I gather the Texas incident has been settled. I mean, it's been several years. Albert's not going to jail or anything."

"Nothing happened!" Anita blazed. "Good God, Tess, you can't believe that Albert would do a thing like that!"

"I'm merely reporting what I heard, Anita."

"Homosexual advances!" Anita snapped. "That's what those vicious boys said. They were troublemakers, those two. Always causing problems at school. When Albert finally had to suspend them for a week — after repeated warnings — they told their parents he'd made advances to them in his office, fondled their private parts!"

"Oh, dear." Tess could think of nothing else to say.

"It was the cruelest revenge they could think of, and it worked," Anita went on. "Their parents went to the school board, and Albert was called in for a meeting with the board, the two teenage boys, and their parents. It was his word against theirs, and one of the fathers was an influential citizen. Albert had a sterling record prior to that, but the board members were a bunch of cowards and refused to stand behind him. The superintendent, a totally political animal if there ever was one, took the boys' side, too. One of the board members told Albert privately that he thought the boys were lying, but there was nothing he could do about it."

"Anita, I'm so sorry."

"If we both could have worked another six years, our retirement income would have been twice what it is now. We could have bought an RV and traveled for several months out of the year. That was our plan, but it was destroyed by the lies of two teenage boys. We couldn't stay in that town after the rumors got around, so I had to give up my job, too. We even had to take a loss on our house."

"Oh, Anita . . ." There was such despair and resentment in the woman's voice that Tess had no idea how to comfort her.

"We moved to Victoria Springs because of the center and the low-income housing," Anita went on.

And because nobody there knew them or the dark rumors they'd left behind in Texas, Tess added silently.

"Edwina was one of the first people I met," Anita went on. "I was so lonely, and she couldn't have been sweeter. Boy, was I fooled!"

"You confided in her?"

Anita nodded. "I'd known her several months and we'd spent a lot of time together. I knew by then that she was eccentric, but she'd never been unkind to me. I noticed that she seemed to have a lot of differences with other people at the center, though, and I should have realized she wasn't all that she seemed to be with Albert and me. But I was so starved for a friend . . ."

Tess nodded. "You were vulnerable, and Edwina took advantage of that. I understand."

Anita's hands clenched and unclenched in her lap. "One day I invited Edwina to the apartment for dinner. Albert was out, playing cards with some men he'd met at the center. They ate at a restaurant, then went to somebody's house. After dinner, Edwina and I had a couple of drinks, and Edwina confided in me about her marriage to Gerald Bates. According to her, the divorce was all Mercy's fault — she wouldn't leave Gerald alone. Later I realized that Edwina had probably twisted the truth, but then I believed every word."

"According to Mercy, Edwina tricked Gerald into marrying her by telling him she was pregnant. Then, after they were married, she told him she'd lost the baby."

"It figures." Anita sighed heavily. "If only I'd known then . . . but I didn't. I'm not accustomed to alcohol, so I guess the drinks loosened my tongue, and I told Edwina what happened in Texas." The ploy that had worked with Gerald Bates seemed to have worked as well with Anita. "Less than two weeks later," Anita went on, "Edwina began asking Albert to make repairs on her house."

"And when he refused, she threatened to tell your secret," Tess finished for her.

"Oh, she never came right out and said it that bluntly. She'd say things like, 'I hope that distasteful business in Texas never gets out here.' Or 'Did you see that business on TV, that child care worker being accused of molesting children in Connecticut? Even if she gets off at trial, she'll have to leave town.' Edwina left no doubt about what she meant."

Tess was beginning to understand that Edwina's dark side was much blacker than she'd imagined. As she turned in at the center and drove around to park in front of the McBrooms' apartment, she said, "Edwina wasn't well liked by anybody in Victoria

Springs that I've talked to. Perhaps you should have called her bluff, let her talk. If it was untrue —"

Anita snatched her quilting book from the floor and wrenched open the car door. The look she gave Tess was hot enough to singe facial hair. "You see? Even you don't believe me!"

"I didn't mean to imply that, Anita. Honestly. I only meant that somebody like Edwina couldn't really hurt you by spreading rumors. I mean, people would surely consider the source. Think of the lies told about celebrities in the tabloids, and they learn to ignore them."

Anita stared at her as if she were dim-witted. "Apparently you've never been the target of that kind of vicious lie, Tess. The worst thing anyone can say about a person is that you molest children."

Tess recalled stories she'd seen on the television news about convicted child molesters being turned loose into communities where the citizens were campaigning to force them to move on. She'd understood the citizens' concern. If she'd lived there with children, she might well have been out carrying placards with the others. But what if the target of all that outrage had been wrongly convicted? A pitiful image of Alfred being subjected to pickets and threats in Victoria Springs sprang into her mind. The thought was deeply troubling.

"Most people don't bother trying to find out if there's any truth to the stories," Anita told her. "They get hysterical. People you thought were your friends won't talk to you. They cross the street to keep from having to acknowledge your existence. They don't want you in their town."

"I'm terribly sorry, Anita."

She climbed out of the car. "It doesn't help," she said flatly. "Please don't repeat what I've told you."

"I won't, but I can't promise what Butts might do." Tess was still debating with herself whether to even tell Butts what she'd learned about Albert McBroom. She would hate to make the McBrooms' life even worse than it was. On the other hand, they'd certainly had a strong motive to want Edwina out of their lives for good. Of course Butts had to be told. "Anita, it might be best if Albert went to Chief Butts and explained to him what happened and how Edwina used it against him."

Standing beside the car, the door still open, Anita hugged the quilting book to her chest. "It just goes on and on," she said hopelessly. "Two hateful juvenile delinquents tell a lie about you, and it throws a cloud over the rest of your life." She shut the door and shuffled into her apartment, her shoulders slumped.

Tess felt so sorry for the woman that she could have cried. Did the boys really lie? She wanted to believe that because she liked Albert McBroom. She was certain of one thing. Anita believed her husband.

15

When Tess got back to the center, Jenny called to her from the kitchen. "Your cousin Cinny phoned and left a message," Jenny said. "Three guesses."

Tess laughed. "I never know what Cinny will come up with next. I give up."

"Cinny is going to be at the meeting at the savings and loan this afternoon."

"Cinny is in Edwina's will, too?"

Jenny nodded. "Isn't that incredible? Cinny was stunned. Like us, she's trying to figure out what token Edwina might have bequeathed to her. She's hoping it's something small, like a figurine, something she can keep in her bookshop. Why do you think Cinny's included?"

"Hmmm," Tess mused. "Cinny did give Edwina books for the book discussions when she couldn't find them at the library. It sounds like Edwina left a little something to everybody who was in any way kind to her."

Jenny's brown brows lifted. "I've thought about it, Tess, and I can't imagine Edwina had anything to leave us, besides that trash in her house. Sounds like the three of us could be going through Edwina's stuff together."

Gathered in the meeting room at the savings and loan were Tess, Cinny, Jenny, and the Hectors. Glancing around, Tess wondered if this handful of people mentioned in Edwina's will were the only ones who had accommodated her when she needed a favor, earning a special place in her life. Skip, of course, was related, but none of the others could really be described as a friend of Edwina's. It was sad, but as Tess reminded herself, Edwina had managed to alienate most of the people who would have been her friends, given half a chance.

Silver-haired James Fillbrook, the attorney, was a tall, distinguished-looking man wearing an expensive pinstriped Italian suit. Tess had not expected Edwina's attorney to be so — well, so successful. She'd have thought Edwina would have found somebody cheap.

Fillbrook sat at the head of the conference table where the beneficiaries were gathered. A leather briefcase adorned with brass initials lay on the table before him.

"It looks as if we're all here now," he said as he snapped open the case and took out a file folder. Opening the folder, he extracted a legal-sized document and glanced around the table. "I have copies of the will for all of you, which I'll hand out after the reading. Now, let's get down to business." He dropped his eyes to the will and began to read. "I, Edwina Gail Riley, of Victoria Springs, Missouri, make this my Will and revoke all prior Wills and Codicils. I appoint James Fillbrook, attorney-at-law, Springfield, Missouri, as personal representative of this will and my estate. My personal representative may pay expenses of my last illness and funeral, claims, costs of administration, and taxes assessed by reason of my death as my personal representative shall in his discretion deem necessary or desirable."

While the legalese droned on, Tess took a quick look around the table. Cinny and Jenny were watching the attorney with eager interest. Tess could almost read their thoughts: *Get to the bequests. The curiosity is killing me.*

When Fillbrook began reading the will, Skip Hector had shifted forward in his chair, his arms resting on the table, hands clasped tightly. His full attention was on the attorney. Tess had detected a certain tension in Skip from the moment she, Cinny, and Jenny had entered the room together. He seemed less than happy and a little suspicious when he saw who the other heirs were.

Milly, on the other hand, was leaning back in her chair, her eyes on Skip, as if she was more interested in gauging his reactions than in learning the details of Edwina's will.

"I'm skipping now to the bequests," Fillbrook said finally. "You all will be able to read the full text of the will later."

Tess returned her attention to the attorney. He cleared his throat and went on, "To my friend Hyacinthe Forrest, of Victoria Springs, Missouri, for her kindnesses, I leave the sum of one hundred dollars. To my friend Tess Darcy, of Victoria Springs, Missouri, for her kindnesses, I leave the sum of one hundred dollars."

Tess and Cinny exchanged relieved smiles. They wouldn't have to go through Edwina's belongings after all. And considering Edwina's obvious poverty, one hundred dollars was a generous gift. Tess thought she'd probably give hers to charity. The sad thing was that Edwina had considered two casual acquaintances her friends.

"To Jenny Vercourt, director of the Senior Citizens Center in Victoria Springs, Missouri," Fillbrook went on, "who has provided me with a home away from home during my retirement years, I leave twenty-five percent of the sum total of my investment accounts."

Jenny stirred and frowned. Tess could almost hear her thinking, *What investment accounts?*

"And to my nephew, Steven 'Skip' Hector, of Fort Worth, Texas, I leave the full amount in my checking account at the First National Bank of Victoria Springs, Missouri, and the property at 406 Ninth Street, Victoria Springs, Missouri, including the house and all the contents. In addition, I leave Steven 'Skip' Hector seventy-five percent of my investment accounts."

Milly was looking bumfuzzled. Skip frowned and opened his mouth to speak, but the attorney raised a hand. "I can't give you the exact amount in Ms. Riley's accounts, as the investment accounts are mostly in equities and various bond and fixed-income funds. However, I phoned Ms. Riley's investment advisor earlier today, and he gave me a close estimate. The bequests will not be available to you, of course, until the will is probated."

"How long will that take?" Skip asked.

Fillbrook's elegant brows lifted a fraction. "It could take two or three months. If we're very lucky, we can get it through the court in six weeks. I'll try to move it along."

"How much are you going to charge us for this?" Skip asked, his tone surly.

Fillbrook eyed him disdainfully. "Ms. Riley opened a separate account at my bank in my name and hers. There's enough in the account to cover the legal fees in connection with the probate. Ms. Riley didn't want them to come out of the beneficiaries' shares." He reached into the briefcase again and placed a stack of legal-sized papers on the table. "Here are copies of the will." He glanced at Tess, then Cinny. "Ms. Darcy and Ms. Forrest, I'd like to speak to the remaining heirs in private, please. Mrs. Hector, you may leave or stay, as you wish."

"I'll stay," Milly said.

After taking copies of the will, Tess and

Cinny left the room. Outside, Cinny whispered, "What do you think that's about?"

"He's probably going to tell them more about those accounts. It was clever of Edwina to mention percentages and not the dollar amounts in her will. Wills are public records, but Edwina's won't reveal how much she really had."

Cinny shrugged. "Which, let's face it, can't be much. I think Edwina just liked intrigue."

Tess was frowning. "I don't know. She had *investment* accounts."

A few minutes later, Jenny and the Hectors exited the meeting room. Jenny's face was pale, as if she'd received a severe shock. Skip appeared bewildered and stalked past Tess and Cinny, muttering churlishly. As for Milly, she looked as if she'd been punched in the stomach.

Jenny grabbed Tess's arm. "Come on, let's get out of here." Tess and Cinny hurried to keep up with her as she left the savings and loan building and headed for the lot where Tess had parked her car.

As they got in, Jenny waved the sheaf of papers clutched in her hand and exploded, "Oh, my God! Oh, my dear God!"

"What?" Cinny asked. She got in back, while Jenny took the front passenger seat. Leaning over the seat to peer at the papers in Jenny's hand, Cinny asked, "What're those papers?"

"It's an inventory of Edwina's investments," Jenny said. "Skip and I are supposed to contact the investment advisor." She stared at the papers again. "I can't believe it!"

"What?" demanded Cinny as Tess started the motor and backed out of the parking place.

"Edwina had about a million in investments," Jenny said.

Tess shot a glance at her passenger. "A million? As in dollars?"

Jenny nodded. "Unbelievable, isn't it?" Suddenly she laughed. The laugh had a near-hysterical edge to it. Jenny was truly stunned by the lawyer's revelation. "I let her take things from the center because I thought she was broke."

Cinny gasped. "You get twenty-five percent! That means you get two hundred and fifty thousand!"

Jenny sucked in a deep breath. "I still can't believe it. There must be some mistake."

"I don't think Fillbrook would make that kind of mistake," Tess said. "I'm sure he checked Edwina's accounts when she made the will."

"Wow!" Cinny said, still marveling over Jenny's good fortune. After a long silence in which Tess and Cinny digested the amazing information that Edwina Riley had been a millionaire, Cinny said, "What I can't believe is that I gave that woman books because she said she couldn't afford to buy them."

"That was Edwina," Tess said. "She never got rid of anything — and apparently that included money."

"She was a cheapskate," Cinny said.

"Well, she appreciated the books, Cinny," Tess told her. "She left you a hundred bucks." Tess laughed. "She called us her friends and left us a measly hundred dollars. Jenny, she must have thought of you as a daughter."

"But she lied!" Cinny said, still outraged.

Tess drove out of the savings and loan parking lot. "The way she lived, her whole life was a lie," she said.

"Those awful macaroni and cheese dishes she brought to the potlucks," Jenny said. "And those ancient polyester pantsuits she wore. We all thought she couldn't afford anything else. It's like one of those stories you read in the newspapers. Some old bum dies in a hovel, and they find out he's got a fortune stashed in his mattress."

"At least Edwina was smart enough to hire an investment advisor," Tess said, "and a good lawyer."

Jenny looked at the papers still clutched tightly in her hand. "The investment advisor is in Springfield, too, like the lawyer. Didn't she trust anybody in Victoria Springs?"

"Yeah," Cinny agreed. "I'd put Luke up against any investment advisor anywhere. And Cody's not a bad lawyer, either."

"I imagine she didn't want anybody in Victoria Springs to know she had money to invest," Tess said. "The way she skimped and cut corners, I certainly never suspected."

"My head's still reeling," Jenny said. "Oh! We'll have enough to pay off the center and remodel the kitchen and get totally out of debt!"

"Don't forget taxes," Tess said.

"Even if we have to pay a third of it to the IRS, we'll have about enough left to do all that." Jenny expelled a loud breath. "I feel like I just won the lottery." After a thoughtful pause, she added, "Where did Edwina get a million dollars?"

Tess had been mulling over the same question. Could the money have been hush money? Perhaps Edwina had been blackmailing people for a long time. "Maybe the investment advisor can tell you," she said. "But a more important question, under the circumstances, is who knew she was worth a fortune?"

Cinny sucked in a loud breath and leaned forward from the back seat to thrust her head between the other two. "The nephew. He's the only one who could have known. And he's the one who profits most from her death. Did you see that look he got on his face when the lawyer said Jenny got twenty-five percent?"

"And that was before he knew how much that was," Jenny told them.

"Maybe not," Tess mused. "Maybe Edwina told him."

"I don't think so," Jenny said. "You should have seen him when the lawyer gave us these printouts and he realized what Edwina was worth. He was okay with the hundred-dollar bequests, but he was mad as hell about my share, and he didn't bother hiding it. He kept saying it wasn't fair, wasn't right. His wife kept telling him to shut up."

"It wouldn't surprise me," Cinny put in, "if he filed a lawsuit, claiming Jenny coerced Edwina or something."

"He did hint something about a lawsuit, but Fillbrook discouraged him. Can he actually sue me?" Jenny asked, alarmed.

"He can sue anybody for anything, if he can get a lawyer to take the case," Cinny said. "With that much money at stake, he can probably find one."

"Oh, no." Jenny sounded deflated. "Then I'll have to hire a lawyer, too. I knew it was too good to be true."

"Don't worry about it," Tess advised. "I don't think he can make a case against you in court. An honest lawyer will tell him that. And if it ever gets to court, everybody at the center will come to your defense."

"Yeah, we'll testify to your sterling character, won't we, Tess?" Cinny asked.

"You bet."

Jenny looked somewhat relieved. "I can't wait to tell Willis," she said. "And then I'm going to call this investment advisor. I have to hear him say how much money is in those accounts before I'll fully believe it."

At the same time that Tess was driving back

to the senior citizens center, the red Honda, with Milly at the wheel, was moving in the direction of Iris House. Since leaving the savings and loan, Skip had been reading through the inventory of investments the attorney had given him. As if he knew anything about stocks and bonds, Milly thought sourly. She had had to practically drag him from the meeting room. He'd wanted to discuss suing Jenny Vercourt for her portion of the inheritance. Fillbrook had, as diplomatically as posssible, suggested that Skip would probably be wasting his money on such a suit. He'd pointed out that Ms. Riley had been in command of all her faculties when she made the will, which had been properly drawn up and witnessed. Nevertheless, Skip had persisted until the attorney finally told him that he'd have to find another attorney since Fillbrook, as Edwina's personal representative, was charged with seeing that her wishes were carried out. Representing one heir in a suit against another heir would be a conflict of interest.

"That bitch tricked Aunt Edwina somehow," Skip grumbled from the passenger seat. "You saw how she was at the center — like butter wouldn't melt in her mouth."

"Get real, Skip!" Milly retorted. "Forget trying to get Jenny Vercourt's share. Can you see anybody putting something over on Edwina?"

Skip scowled at her. "She was old and alone."

"But not senile. Edwina was as wily as they come. I doubt that anybody ever tricked her in her life. Give it up, Skip. You're not going to get Jenny Vercourt's share. If you try, you could end up spending all your inheritance on lawyers and have nothing to show for it."

"I just can't believe Aunt Edwina did that to me," he snarled. "It's not right."

Milly groaned. "Lay off that, okay? Edwina had the right to leave what she had to anybody she wanted. She didn't have to leave you a dime. My God, I thought you'd be jumping through hoops. You're rich, Skip."

"Not yet. If I know lawyers, Fillbrook will drag out the probate for as long as possible so he can hike his fees."

"He said Edwina had already given him enough to cover his fees." They rode in silence for several moments. Milly couldn't help smiling. "Edwina seems to have thought of everything."

"Yeah, but I'd love to know how much is in that joint account she had with Fillbrook. How do I know it's not another million?"

Milly rolled her eyes. "I'm sure he'll have to file all the records with the probate court. The judge will determine if Fillbrook's fees are inordinately high." Skip didn't respond, and after a moment she asked, "Where do you suppose Edwina got that kind of money?"

"Investments," Skip said crossly.

"But you have to have money to invest in the first place," Milly pointed out. "Where'd she get it?"

Skip sighed. "I don't know, and I don't care."

After several more moments of silence, Milly had to say what was really on her mind or she'd burst. "You knew, didn't you?"

"Knew what?"

"You knew she had a lot of money."

She felt Skip's eyes on her, but she didn't glance toward him.

"How the hell could I have known? She lived like she was the next thing to homeless. Didn't even replace that old Ford she drove for years when it finally gave up the ghost. Got other people to haul her around. Geez, how could anybody have known?"

"You went through everything in her house. She must have had some records, maybe reports on her investments."

"There was nothing like that in the house, not even a copy of her will. Fillbrook told me she had a safe-deposit box at his bank in Springfield, the one where she opened that account with him. She kept all her records there. Fillbrook's name was on the box, too. She even left her key with a bank officer. She rarely opened the box; she mailed stuff to Fillbrook, and he'd put it in the box. He's already cleaned it out and turned in the key. Like he was in a big hurry to get rid of evidence or something. Seems pretty suspicious to me."

When Milly didn't respond, he prompted, "Milly?"

"What?"

"I thought she probably had a small savings account. I didn't know about the investments. You believe me, don't you?"

She sighed. "I'm trying to, Skip."

But the fact was, she was finding that hard to do. All the doubts about Skip that she'd been having the last few days had coalesced into one haunting question. Was Skip a murderer?

16

Within two days, the news of Edwina's million-dollar estate had gotten out at the center. Jenny swore she hadn't told anybody but Willis, who, she said, had practically fainted at the news. He'd had to sit down, then had asked her to repeat what she'd just said. She and Willis had agreed to keep quiet about it until the will was probated. She suspected that one of the seniors may have heard her and Willis talking about it and spread it around. They'd talked of little else since Jenny learned about her inheritance, she admitted.

Edwina Riley had been a millionaire, and nobody in Victoria Springs had suspected. That was the main topic of conversation at the center. Reactions ranged from amazement to anger.

"To think," Anita whispered to Tess as the sewing circle broke up on Wednesday, "Edwina was pressuring Albert to do her home repairs for free — and injure his back further — while she had all that money in investments. It makes me so mad I could kill her, if she wasn't already dead." When she realized what she'd said, she caught her breath, put a hand on Tess's arm, and whispered urgently, "I didn't mean that the way it sounded, Tess. You know I would never do anything like that."

Tess murmured an agreement, but ever since she'd learned about Edwina's fortune, she wasn't sure about a lot of things. What if Anita and Albert had somehow learned about the money? They'd have been totally outraged, knowing Edwina could well afford to pay for repairs but instead was blackmailing Albert into doing them as the price of her silence. That, added to Albert's forced retirement and their resulting meager income, might have pushed one of them over the edge. But Edwina had been so secretive about her money. It was hard to imagine how the McBrooms could have found out.

The seniors were still talking about Edwina's estate at lunch. Tess had carried her tray to the table where Ross Dellin, Joyce Banaker, and Jenny Vercourt were sitting.

"If I'd known the old hag was worth that much," Ross was saying as Tess sat down, "I'd have *sold* her that damned locker."

Jenny gave Ross an odd look. "Don't say things like that, Ross," she cautioned.

"Hell, Jenny, you know I'm just running off at the mouth," Ross grumbled.

Jenny continued to study him for a moment, her expression speculative. She seemed to have something on her mind, something to do with Ross. Tess wished she knew what.

Ross seemed different since Edwina's death, less angry, more subdued. Maybe he was wondering who he would fuss and fight with now. But watching him lower his head and pick up his fork, after Jenny's reprimand, Tess wondered if there could have been more between Edwina and Ross than had appeared on the surface.

Yesterday Desmond Butts had come to the center with the information that Ross's fingerprints were all over the outside of Edwina's sewing box. Ross's response had been, "Of course they were! She was always putting that box in my locker and I was always taking it out again!" Jenny and Tess had backed him up.

Nobody's prints but Edwina's had been found on the contents of the sewing box. A print on Mercy's ring had been too smudged to be identified. Butts had confided to Tess that all the quilting needles had been dipped in poison, but there were no identifiable prints on them, either. Not surprising, since they were so small. Fragments of prints were on two needles. According to the lab, they could have been Edwina's, but there wasn't enough of the prints present for them to confirm it.

After much consideration, Tess asked Butts if Albert McBroom had been in to talk to him. When Butts said no, Tess told him what had happened to the McBrooms in Texas, adding that Anita had confided in Edwina, who had used it to pressure Albert into doing her home repairs. Butts had clearly not known any of it. Later Butts had interviewed the McBrooms in their apartment, apparently learning nothing new. But Tess would bet the McBrooms had gone up a few notches on Butts's list of murder suspects.

Somebody had planned and carried out a murder right under the noses of the people at the center. Whoever it was had been careful enough not to leave any fingerprints. This knowledge did not give Tess any hunches about the killer's identity. With all the TV cop and lawyer shows, everybody knew about fingerprints.

Tess remained silent, picking at her food and thinking, while her tablemates continued to talk about Edwina's will. Now that she knew of Edwina's fortune, Tess was seeing everybody differently — even Mercy, who had told her that Edwina acted as if she had a big secret, something that nobody else knew. That chance remark now seemed suspect.

After talking to Edwina's investment counselor, Jenny had reported to Tess that Edwina had started investing over forty years ago, beginning with only a few thousand dollars. Thereafter she deposited with the investment firm up to a thousand dollars a month from her salary plus all the overtime pay she earned through the years. She had never removed a dollar from the accounts. Edwina had pinched every penny, denied herself a single small luxury, refused to pay for necessary repairs to her house, in order to keep investing. After retiring, she'd continued to live at the poverty level rather than dip into her savings.

And Edwina didn't even have children to leave it to. There was, Tess decided, something very skewed about that kind of thinking. Wasn't it Mercy who'd said that Edwina had a sickness? Perhaps Mercy had known about Edwina's big secret all along. Even so, Tess reminded herself, it didn't give Mercy a motive, for she had not profited from Edwina's death.

Unless . . . Suppose Edwina started her investment program with money she got from Gerald in the divorce, while Gerald and Mercy had started their life together with nothing.

All the "what ifs" and "supposes" were giving Tess a headache. She tried to push them aside and attend to the table conversation.

"You all heard Edwina tell me that she couldn't pay the towing bill, that I couldn't get blood out of a turnip," Joyce was saying indignantly. "All the time she was sitting on a million dollars!"

"Yeah," Ross agreed, "and remember how she always tried to get the books for our discussions from the library because she said she had no money for books?"

Joyce nodded. "I'm going to pursue this. I'll

mail a statement for the towing bill to Edwina's lawyer."

"Lotsa luck," Ross growled. "It wasn't Edwina's car that was towed, and she denied reporting it as abandoned. Lawyers don't shell out money from an estate without proof that you're a legitimate creditor."

"But I am a legitimate creditor," Joyce fumed.

"Can you prove it?" Ross asked.

Joyce's determined expression faded as she thought about it, and she looked deflated. "I know Edwina reported the car, but no, I can't really prove it."

"Then don't waste a stamp," Ross advised.

Thursday morning, Skip was standing at the window of the guest parlor, deep in thought, when Tess left her apartment to go to the kitchen.

His expression reminded Tess of the way he'd looked when she'd found him sitting alone in the kitchen late at night. What had he been doing there? Staying out of the bedroom to keep from disturbing Milly? Or was there more to it than that? Tess had a sudden, dreadful thought. Had Skip been waiting to make sure he'd have the kitchen to himself for a good while so he could brew up some poison? As Cinny had pointed out, Skip had certainly profited from Edwina's death.

Sensing another presence, Skip turned

around. "Oh, hello, Tess."

"You're up early," she said. "I'll make coffee right away. Breakfast should be ready in fifteen minutes or so."

"Good," Skip replied, following her to the kitchen. "I'm going to put Aunt Edwina's house on the market, so I need to start clearing it out today. Do you know somebody who would haul off her belongings?"

"No, but check the phone book under trash haulers." Tess got out the coffee and measured the correct amount into the automatic drip coffeemaker. That done, she found Gertie's pancake recipe and got out the mixing bowl and the ingredients she would need. "You might be able to sell Edwina's magazine collection to a used-book dealer. If I were you I'd get a couple of dealers to look at what's there before you have everything hauled away."

"You really think the magazines could be worth something?"

"I don't know much about it," Tess said, measuring out flour and then milk, "but I've heard that old copies of certain magazines, like *Life*, have become collectors' items."

"I guess I better check it out then."

"Edwina was so tight-fisted," Tess said, "I'm surprised she would spend money on magazines."

"She didn't," Skip told her. "I looked through one of those stacks in her living room. The mailing labels all have other people's names on them. She must have scavenged them from trash barrels."

Tess found she could easily picture Edwina doing that.

Skip groaned. "God, I hate having to deal with that mess. Milly refused to go with me, so looks like I'll have to handle it by myself." He walked over to the coffeemaker. "Can I pour out of this before it's through dripping?"

"It'll stop when you remove the pot," Tess said. "Go ahead. The mugs are in that cabinet over the coffeemaker." While she mixed the pancake batter and set the griddle on the range to heat, Skip took his coffee into the dining room.

While Skip's pancakes browned, Tess put bacon in the microwave to cook. Skip was seated at the end of the dining table, staring out the window, when she set out place mats, plates, silverware, and napkins.

"Did you have any idea Edwina had that kind of money?" Tess asked.

He turned from the window. "Not a clue."

Was he lying? Tess tried to read his expression but couldn't. She went back to the kitchen and ladled the pancakes onto a plate, piling the bacon beside them. She arranged the food, syrup pitcher, and butter on a tray and carried it to the dining room, setting it down where Skip could reach it.

Skip took three pancakes and started spreading butter on them. "Do the police have any idea who poisoned Aunt Edwina?"

"Not that I've heard. What do you think?"

He glanced at her sharply. "From what I saw at the senior citizens center, Aunt Edwina seemed to have made a lot of enemies. And that poison — you can buy it at pharmaceutical houses. But you could make your own, too. It comes from castor bean seeds. Anybody could get hold of them."

Tess stared at him as he poured syrup over the stack of pancakes on his plate. "Actually, I saw some in Edwina's front yard."

"I hadn't noticed." He cut a triangle of pancakes, chewed it slowly.

"How did you know ricin came from castor beans?"

His glanced at her, his eyes wide with what could have been innocence. It also could have been guile. "I looked it up. Found a book on poisonous plants in your library."

It was entirely possible there was such a book in the library. Tess had inherited her Aunt Iris's books along with the house, and Iris had had quite a collection of reference works on flowers and plants. She would check later to be sure.

"The book said that the beans would have to be ground up or something to be fatal."

The fact that Edwina's needles had been drenched in the poison wasn't yet common knowledge. So either Skip didn't know how Edwina got the poison or he was clever enough to let Tess think he didn't know.

"But we all ate the same food that Edwina ate at the potluck," Tess said. "So how could ground-up castor beans have been in her food? Besides, according to the medical examiner, Edwina didn't eat the poison. She got it through her skin, through a cut or something."

Skip stared at her for a moment, then shrugged. "Chief Butts told me what had killed her, but he didn't mention that. Well, I don't guess it matters how she got it in her system — it killed her." He watched Tess as he said this. Did he really not know about the needles? If he did, he wasn't about to admit it, since the only way he could know was if he'd soaked the needles in the poison himself.

Tess retreated to the kitchen. She poured herself a cup of coffee and drank it at the kitchen table, waiting for Skip to finish his breakfast and leave the house. As soon as he was gone, she took the staircase to the second floor, then the spiral staircase to the library in the tower.

Tess hadn't read much since she'd started volunteering at the senior citizens center, so she hadn't been up to the tower for a few weeks. It was spotlessly clean, as usual; Gertie dusted it regularly, even during the off-season when there were no guests to make use of it. The white wicker furniture with green-and-lavender flowered chintz cushions, the four sections of floor-to-ceiling bookshelves, and the tall, curving windows that looked down on the backyard made the library a favorite retreat of Tess's. She regretted that she hadn't found an hour or two lately to curl up there with a book and a cup of tea.

Perhaps later today, she thought, as she went to the nonfiction section of the bookshelves. She'd placed Aunt Iris's books on the bottom three shelves. She bent to scan titles and pulled out *Common Poisonous Plants.* Turning to the index at the back of the book, she found "Castor Bean," flipped to the pages listed, and scanned the entry. The information was all there. Skip could have read the entry, Tess admitted as she returned the book to its place on the shelf.

But, she mused, the question was when had he read it? After Butts told him what had killed Edwina? Or before Edwina was poisoned?

Tess left the tower, and, as she was passing the Annabel Jane room, the door opened and Milly peered out. She was dressed in jeans and a gray sweatshirt. "Is Skip still downstairs?"

"No, he said he was going to Edwina's house to start sorting through her things."

Milly stepped into the hall, closing the door behind her. "I guess it's safe to come out then. He thinks I should help him, and I didn't want to get into another argument about it. Not before I have some coffee anyway."

She followed Tess downstairs. In the kitchen, Tess filled a mug with coffee and handed it to

Milly. "I'll have your pancakes ready in a few minutes."

Milly leaned against the work island in the center of the kitchen, sipping her coffee and watching Tess. "We're a bother to you, with your cook gone and all."

The batter sizzled as Tess poured three disks on the hot griddle. "It's no bother," she said. "Really." She glanced at Milly and smiled. "I'm just sorry all this had to happen on your honeymoon."

Milly frowned as she lifted the mug and took another sip of coffee. Then she set the mug on the counter. "I'm finished with lies," she said.

Tess threw her a questioning look.

"We're not on our honeymoon," Milly went on.

"Oh." Tess hardly knew what to say. "Well, that's your business — yours and Skip's."

"We're not even married," Milly continued, as if once started, she wanted to get it all out. "It was Skip's idea to say we were on our honeymoon. He said Edwina wouldn't let us sleep together in her house if she knew we weren't married."

Knowing that Edwina had tricked Gerald Bates into marrying her by sleeping with him, Tess thought that Edwina had hardly been in a position to pass judgment. However, that wouldn't have stopped her.

"After one night in Edwina's spare bedroom," Milly was saying, "I refused to stay there." She grimaced. "So we came here."

Tess could certainly understand Milly's reluctance to stay at Edwina's, but why hadn't they rented a room in the first place? Since they were willing to lie anyway, they could have told Edwina they'd taken two rooms.

As if reading Tess's thoughts, Milly said, "Skip hadn't seen his aunt in quite a while. In fact, he'd hardly mentioned her. Then, out of the blue, he gets this brainstorm that we have to come to Victoria Springs and Edwina has to meet me. I was supposed to make her like me." She shook her head, as if at the absurdity of that idea. "Skip is out of a job and flat broke, and I didn't want to put anything else on my credit card. So he came up with the idea that we'd tell Edwina we were on our honeymoon, so we could share a room at her house." She walked over to the coffeemaker and refilled her mug. Turning around, she said, "The few hours we spent at Edwina's house were awful. Maybe I shouldn't say it now that she's gone, but the woman drove me crazy. She was a nut. She actually told me how much water to run into the tub for a bath. Two inches and no more. Can you believe that? And she rattled on about how she was going to teach me to crochet and quilt, raved about how she loved to quilt, said she had scars on her fingers from it because she couldn't use a thimble. I knew I couldn't take another night with Edwina, even if her house hadn't been such a disaster. So we used my credit card after all."

Tess fixed an expression of casual interest on her face, while taking note that Skip and Milly had known that Edwina didn't use a thimble. And they'd both been at the center a couple of times. They'd had access to Edwina's sewing box.

Milly took a swallow of coffee. "I told Skip last night that he had to pay me back for our stay here once he gets Edwina's money. I never wanted to come to Victoria Springs in the first place, but Skip wheedled until I gave in. Boy, the way things have turned out, I wish I hadn't listened to him."

Tess ladled the pancakes onto a plate. "You can eat here or in the dining room."

"I'll eat here," Milly decided. Tess set the plate on the kitchen table, then got silverware, napkin, and the syrup, butter, and bacon from the dining room table.

While Milly ate, Tess put Skip's dishes in the dishwasher and wiped the range. "It was an odd time for Skip to decide to take a trip," she ventured finally, "I mean if he was broke."

Milly didn't answer for a moment. Then she said with studied casualness, "That's what I thought, but he said Edwina was his only living relative and she wasn't getting any younger. When Skip gets one of his harebrained schemes, there's no reasoning with him."

And he wanted to make sure Edwina was leaving him an inheritance, Tess thought, remembering that earlier breakfast conversation between Skip and Milly. According to Jenny, he'd been furious when he learned Edwina hadn't left him every niggling little dime, to use Milly's phrase. Still, Skip's share would be a sizable sum, certainly more money than he'd ever had in his life or probably ever hoped to have.

"Did Skip have any idea how large an estate Edwina had accumulated?" Tess asked.

Milly didn't answer immediately. She made a circle in the syrup on her plate with her fork before she said, "He swears he didn't."

So Milly had asked him, Tess mused.

Abruptly Milly put down her fork, left her pancakes half-eaten, and pushed back her chair. "The pancakes are great, Tess, but I guess I'm not very hungry. I'm going to finish my coffee upstairs. I'll bring the mug back down later."

"No hurry," Tess told her. She finished putting the kitchen to rights, thinking about Milly's response to her question. *He swears he didn't,* she'd said, and there was something in her tone that made Tess think Milly wasn't sure Skip had told her the truth.

17

Later at the center, Jenny called Tess into her office and shut the door. "Guess what Willis heard at the coffee shop this morning."

"Does it have something to do with the murder?"

Jenny nodded, her eyes grave.

"No telling then, the way rumors fly in this town."

"This was straight from the horse's mouth — or almost," Jenny said. "Two police officers were talking in the booth next to Willis's, and he overheard one of them saying that all of Edwina's quilting needles were soaked in poison." She paused, waiting for Tess's reaction.

"If Chief Butts hears about this, those officers are in trouble."

"You don't seem very surprised, Tess."

"Butts told me about the needles the other day. He asked me to keep it confidential. Apparently he forgot to caution his officers."

"I'm sure they weren't aware that Willis could hear them," Jenny said.

"Still, they shouldn't be discussing confidential police business in a public place."

Jenny shrugged. "You know it's impossible to keep a secret for long in Victoria Springs, but I'll tell Willis not to mention it to anybody else. I'm worried, Tess. This means the murderer is somebody at the center, somebody who knew Edwina well enough to know she didn't use a thimble when she quilted."

Tess nodded. "Of course, but the police have assumed all along that it was somebody who frequents the center. You knew that, Jenny."

"Well, yes." Her brow creased worriedly. "But before I heard about the needles, I assumed it was just one theory among several. Now . . ." She ran her hand through her brown hair, a nervous gesture. "I guess I was still hoping Edwina was poisoned somewhere else, that the killer was somebody" — she waved toward the office window — "out there. Somebody not connected to the center."

Tess shook her head. "I wish it had turned out that way, for your and Willis's sake."

Jenny raked both hands through her hair this time. "Just when we learn we'll have the money to renovate the kitchen and make needed repairs on the center and the apartments . . ." She sighed heavily. "We have to face facts, Tess. There is no longer any doubt. We have a killer in our midst." She shuddered.

Put so bluntly, it made Tess feel like shuddering, too.

"Willis says," Jenny went on, "we could still have problems with the state or federal government. We could still get closed down. People in town are talking already."

"You'd have more to worry about if Edwina had died of food poisoning from something she ate here. As it is, I don't think there's much danger of your being closed down, Jenny."

"Honestly?" She peered into Tess's eyes, as if seeking reassurance.

"This is the only senior citizens center in town," Tess went on. "And now that you'll have the money to fix it up, the inspectors will see you're meeting all the regulations. Once the investigation is over, the talk will die down. People will forget."

"I hope you're right, Tess. Still, I have to go along with Willis. He says we shouldn't start the repairs right away. We don't want to pour money into this place if there's even a small chance we might lose it."

Tess had to agree that at this point caution was called for. "That sounds sensible."

When Tess returned to Iris House a little after four, she phoned the police station and asked for Butts.

"What is it, Tess?" Butts barked into the phone.

"I was wondering if you've done any more checking on the McBrooms."

"Not necessary. They're no longer suspects."

"What!" Although Tess felt sorry for Anita, she still felt that along with Skip the McBrooms had the best motive for killing Edwina. "I know you questioned them at length. I assumed you were trying to put together a case against them."

"I was, but they insisted on taking a lie detector test. I got a guy to come over from Springfield to administer it."

"They passed?"

"With flying colors. I had the tester ask them about that trouble in Texas, too. According to him, they're innocent on both counts."

"How interesting," Tess murmured.

"I've got to go, Tess," Butts said and hung up.

Gazing out the front window, Tess mused that Skip Hector was the only good suspect Butts had left. Noticing that the red Honda wasn't parked in front, Tess wondered suddenly if Skip and Milly had checked out without notifying her. She got the master key from her apartment and peeked into the Annabel Jane Room. The bed was unmade, and several items of clothing were scattered about. Milly's toiletries kit lay open on the dresser. They hadn't left.

As she was descending to the foyer, the young couple came in. Skip, who seemed upset, barely nodded at Tess as he climbed the stairs.

"Is everything all right?" Tess asked Milly.

"I'm not sure," Milly said reflectively. "The

chief of police stopped by Edwina's house while we were there and advised Skip not to leave town without reporting to him first."

Tess knew that Butts told everybody connected to a murder investigation the same thing. It was Butts's way of increasing the pressure in the hope that, given enough time, the killer might crack. She also knew that the only way Butts could legally force a suspect not to leave town was to arrest him. Curiously, many people didn't know that and took Butts's request as an order he was prepared to enforce.

"I'm sure Butts has said the same thing to everybody who was at the center the day Edwina died," Tess said.

Milly cocked her head, as if listening for a faraway sound, and said musingly, "Yeah, but the others live here. They have no reason to leave." The distant look left her eyes as she fixed them on Tess. "Does Chief Butts think Skip killed Edwina?"

"I'm not privy to the Chief's thoughts."

She gazed at Tess for another moment, then headed for the stairs. "I better go up and try to calm Skip down."

Tess heard the telephone ringing in her apartment and hurried to answer it.

"I have something to show you," Luke said. "Is now a good time?"

"Sure," Tess replied. "Can you stay for dinner? I could order in pizza."

"Sounds good. See you in a few minutes."

When Luke arrived, he had a long roll of papers under his arm. Handing the roll to Tess, he took off his coat and threw it over the back of the couch.

"What's this?" Tess asked.

Luke took the roll. "Let's go to the kitchen." Curious but bemused, Tess followed him. He unrolled the papers on the kitchen table, anchoring the corners with the sugar bowl and three heavy mugs from the mug tree on the counter.

"Blueprints?" Tess's eyes flew to his face. Surely he wasn't going to suggest they build a new house. She had thought he understood she couldn't leave Iris House.

Luke took a ballpoint pen from his shirt pocket and used it as a pointer. "I had Tracey Barnes draw the plans. She's the best architect in town. The living room and formal dining room would be here, on the north side, with the new kitchen here." He indicated a wing jutting out behind the dining room.

Tess stared at the blueprints. "New kitchen?"

"I know you love your kitchen, sweetheart, but this one's almost twice as big, and you could make it look just like the old one if you want."

At last understanding dawned as she recalled Luke's tromping around outside in the rain, snapping pictures and making notes. These were plans for an addition to Iris House. "What would we do with the old kitchen?"

"I thought we'd knock out the wall between your sitting room and the kitchen, make it one big den. But if you don't like that idea, Tracey can redraw the plans."

Tess merely nodded and pointed to the plans. "My office would remain where it is now?"

"That's right, and we'd add another bath and a couple of bedrooms in back, which would give us four." He was watching her anxiously.

"I'd lose the bay window in my office," Tess said.

"Yeah. Tracey couldn't figure any way around it. We could put in a skylight, though."

"It's not just the light I'd miss," Tess said. "It's that lovely view of the iris garden."

"Look." Luke pointed to the largest bedroom, one of the two new ones. "Here's the master suite. Practically the whole north wall would be glass, with a door going out to a patio. You'd have an even better view from there." He put a finger under her chin, lifting it so that he could look into her eyes. "You'd lose a little yard, and we'd have to replant some of the iris gardens, but you've got almost two acres here, honey. The lot can easily accommodate a house this large, and you'd still have plenty of yard and garden space."

He looked so earnest. "Oh, Luke, it's wonderful. I know I'd love it. But I can't afford this."

He smiled. "This is going to be my home, too, Tess. I'll pay for the addition." He drew her into his arms. "By the way, Sidney is delirious with the thought of moving into my house. Yesterday I caught him rearranging the living room furniture."

"Rushing things a bit, isn't he?" Tess asked with a laugh.

"That's what I told him when I made him put everything back where it had been."

She sobered. "But Luke, can we possibly have the addition ready by June?"

"I'll give the contractor a first of June deadline. That's no guarantee, of course, but we can build in a penalty if the job's not completed on time. Regardless, we'll manage with your apartment temporarily, if they don't finish before the wedding."

Tess rested her head on his shoulder, taking it all in. It was the perfect solution. She could already picture the master suite, with all those windows providing a view of the gardens. And a bricked patio with chaise longues would be perfect for relaxing on summer evenings.

"Tess?" Luke said after a moment. "Is it okay? Can I start shopping for a contractor?"

"Yes, Luke. And I think Tracey's plans are wonderful." She kissed his cheek. "*You're* wonderful."

"So you finally noticed."

18

Luke left about eleven. Tess had just turned out the lights and gotten in bed when the telephone beside her bed rang.

"Tess, it's Jenny Vercourt. I'm working late at the center. I hope I didn't wake you."

"No, I wasn't asleep yet."

"Willis had to go to Springfield for some supplies," Jenny said, apropos of nothing that Tess could discern. "I told him to stay over. I worry about him falling asleep when he drives at night. Frankly, we haven't slept well the last couple of nights. Too much excitement, I guess. Anyway, with Willis gone, I thought it would be a good chance for me to work late at the center, but the place is chilly and it's beginning to give me the willies. It's creepy here at night." The Vercourts lived in a house a half-mile from the center.

"If you called to hear me tell you your fears are ungrounded, they probably are. But it's late, Jenny. Go home. The work will be there tomorrow."

"That's not why I called."

Jenny's tone worried Tess. "What's wrong, Jenny?"

"I'm not sure what it means, Tess — if it means anything. Maybe I shouldn't be talking to you about it."

"You wouldn't have called if you didn't want to talk to me."

Jenny sighed. "You're right. I haven't even told Willis, because I know he'll want me to keep quiet about it. It could be another black mark against the center. I'm not sure what I should do. I need an objective opinion."

"Okay."

"It's Ross."

"Ross Dellin?"

"Right. It's — Well, let me start at the beginning. The morning of the potluck luncheon I saw Ross getting into Edwina's locker, the one they always fought over."

"He was probably checking to see if she'd moved her things back into it," Tess said. "Remember, he came by at lunch to tell you she'd taken the locker back."

"I wouldn't have given it a second thought except that he had his hand in her sewing box. He put the lid back on it in a hurry when I saw him."

That was problematic, considering what they now knew about the needles. "Are you sure his hand was inside the box?"

"Absolutely. I didn't know about the quilting needles being poisoned then, so I shrugged it off. I figured he was just being nosy, or maybe he was going to take a spool of thread or something to irritate Edwina. I decided to ignore it. I was tired of refereeing their fights over the locker."

"Jenny, if you saw Ross at Edwina's sewing box, that could mean —"

"I know. I've been thinking about it all evening. It means Ross could be the one who poisoned Edwina's needles."

Tess considered it. "I know they fussed a lot, but come on, Jenny. Ross wouldn't commit murder over a locker."

"No, I'm sure he wouldn't. But I found something else when I was emptying the trash baskets at the center today. It's a note. Wait a minute, I'll read it to you. It says, 'Give up the locker in the bottom row and your dirty little secret will remain a secret.' It isn't signed, but I think it's Edwina's handwriting, Tess. I've seen her writing several times on those notes she always made for the book discussions."

So had Tess. Edwina's handwriting was distinctive with spidery curves and squiggles, and the lines on the notes Tess had seen slanted down on the right. "If Edwina wrote it, then it had to be meant for Ross."

"That bit about the locker sure points to him. And remember what he said in the dining room the day of the potluck? He wanted me to know Edwina had switched lockers again. But he also wanted to say that he'd decided to stop fighting with Edwina over the locker and let her have it. I thought that was odd at the time."

"So did I," Tess admitted. "It's not like Ross to give up a good fight. He revels in them."

"The note sounds like blackmail, Tess."

"Another reason to think it's from Edwina," Tess said. "She collected secrets about everybody and then used them to get her way. I wonder what Ross's dirty little secret is?"

"I have no idea, Tess, and he wouldn't tell me."

"You asked him?"

"Yes, I called him."

"When?"

"A few minutes ago. I told him I'd found the note and I was sure it was meant for him. He didn't exactly deny it, either, Tess. Just said Edwina had always been a liar, threatened to sue me for slander if I told anybody else the note was meant for him. Then he hung up on me."

Tess was not surprised. Ross was confrontational, even when he was in the wrong. Especially when he was in the wrong.

"Do you think I should turn the note over to the police," Jenny was asking, "and tell them about seeing Ross nosing around Edwina's sewing box?"

"Yes, I do. It doesn't prove that Ross poisoned the needles, but the police need to have all the available information."

"I was pretty sure that's what you'd say."

Jenny paused and took a deep breath. "I just hate causing trouble for Ross. If he's innocent —" She paused again. "Besides, he can be scary when he's mad."

"I've always thought it was mostly bluster."

"Oh, I know. You're probably right. It's this place at night. I'm going home. I'll talk to the police tomorrow." She paused. "Tess, I think I hear a car out front. Just a minute." She laid down the phone and came back in a few moments. "A car pulled up and parked by the front walk. It's too dark for me to identify it. Oh, Lord, what if it's Ross?"

"It could be anybody, Jenny. Do you have all the doors locked?"

"I think so. Oh, dear, I'd better check. I can slip out the back way. I'll talk to you tomorrow, Tess."

"Jenny, wait!" But she'd hung up.

Tess replaced the receiver. Surely Jenny would not admit anybody to the center at eleven o'clock at night when she was alone there. But Tess wasn't certain. Jenny might admit somebody she knew well — even Ross Dellin. The thought worried Tess. But she told herself her concern was misplaced. Ross Dellin was crochety and rude and had even been known to indulge in verbal abuse, particularly of Don Bob Earling, but that was a long way from causing anybody physical harm.

But would Ross draw the line at physical assault? She remembered how he'd shoved

Edwina out of his way that day in the hall, the day she'd discovered he'd thrown her things out of the locker in the bottom row. If Edwina had fallen, she could have been hurt.

But shoving Edwina in anger was a far cry from carrying out a premeditated murder. Still, worry drove all thought of sleep from Tess's mind. *Stop it,* she told herself, but her thoughts kept coming. Somebody who had already committed one murder might not hesitate to commit a second one.

She stared at the telephone. Finally she picked up the receiver and punched in the number for the police. An officer Tess didn't know answered.

She identifed herself and said, "I was just on the phone with Jenny Vercourt at the senior citizens center. Jenny's there alone, and she told me a car just pulled up in front of the center. Could you send an officer by to make sure she's all right?"

"Yes, ma'am. What's that address?"

Tess told him. He thanked her and hung up. He'd sounded bored, as if he got calls from frightened women frequently. She just hoped he sent a patrol car around right away.

Minutes later, she heard somebody leaving Iris House. Curious, she felt her way through the darkness to the sitting room and peered out the window. Light from the yard lamps revealed Skip getting into the Honda. Now, where could he be going at this time of night?

She paced the apartment for a time. At length, she called the center. After a dozen rings, she gave up and cradled the receiver. Jenny must have gone home. She was probably asleep by now. But Tess made a second call to the police station. "This is Tess Darcy again. Did you have somebody check the senior citizens center?"

"Yes, ma'am," the officer said. "There was an officer in the neighborhood when you called. Everything was closed up, and the place was dark. He checked the door. It was locked."

"Jenny must have gone home then," Tess said.

"Yes, ma'am."

"Was there a car parked in front?"

"No, ma'am."

Evidently Jenny had slipped out the back door, and whoever was in the car parked at the curb had left after getting no response at the front door.

Tess went to bed. After tossing and turning for half an hour, she finally admitted she could not sleep. There were too many questions whirling around in her head. She'd go to the tower for a book. If she could get her mind off the questions, maybe she could fall asleep. She put on a robe and slid her feet into her scuffs, then climbed both sets of stairs quietly, not wanting to disturb Milly.

In the library, she switched on a light and began looking through the fiction shelves, pulling out books to peruse the cover blurbs. She had yet to read at least half the books there, but none of the blurbs grabbed her attention. She wasn't really in the mood for reading; she was too restless.

She returned another book to its place on the shelf. Sitting down on the wicker couch, she stared at the blackness outside the tower windows. A memo pad and several pens lay on the table next to the couch. She picked up the pad and a pen and began doodling. After a moment, she realized she'd been writing Edwina Riley's name over and over.

Maybe if she made a list of murder suspects, she'd see something that had eluded her before. She began to write.

When she stopped to read the list, it contained five names and possible motives. Skip and Milly Hector's names topped the list. (Tess now knew that Milly's name wasn't Hector, but she didn't know what it was. Hector would do for now.) Skip had gained the most from Edwina's death, and his presence in Victoria Springs at the time of the murder seemed almost too coincidental to be believed. Milly could gain from Edwina's death, too, especially if she eventually married Skip.

The other names and motives were:

Mercy Bates. Motive: Edwina told Wally Tanksley something that destroyed Mercy's relationship with Wally, just as Edwina had once tried to destroy Mercy's relationship with Gerald Bates.

Joyce Banaker. Motive: Edwina was waging a harassment campaign against her, and Joyce had vowed to put a stop to it.

Ross Dellin. Motive: Edwina threatened to reveal his "dirty little secret," whatever that was.

She did not add the McBrooms, who'd been cleared by the lie detector tests they'd taken. Tess gnawed the cap of the pen. Edwina may have irritated the Bloom sisters and Don Bob Earling from time to time, but none of the three had profited in any way by Edwina's death, as far as Tess knew. Who else had profited from it?

To be fair, she added another name to the list:

Jenny Vercourt. Motive: Her inheritance of $250,000 from Edwina's estate.

Tess didn't really consider Jenny a serious suspect. Edwina had told Jenny only what she'd told Tess, that she'd left her a little something in her will.

She gnawed the pen cap again. Actually, she had only Jenny's word for what Edwina had told her. What if Jenny had lied? What if she had known that her inheritance would be sizable? Jenny did need money for the repairs on the center. Tess remembered finding her working on the center's accounts, and Jenny had said that no matter how much she juggled the figures, she still could not come up with enough to pay for the new kitchen. Without the inheritance, the Vercourts would have had to take out a loan.

On the other hand, Tess would swear that Jenny's reaction the day the will was read was genuine, that she'd had no idea what Edwina had left her. And tonight on the phone, Jenny had sounded truly concerned about Ross Dellin and torn between keeping quiet and going to the police. Could all that have been an act? Could Jenny have written the note herself to throw suspicion on Ross? She could even have lied about seeing him at Edwina's sewing box.

Tess sighed. Anything was possible, she supposed. But in her gut she did not believe that Jenny Vercourt was a killer. Furthermore, she believed that Jenny was truly stunned when she learned about her inheritance. And Jenny had told Tess that Edwina had left her a little something in her will, which were the exact words Edwina had said to Tess. Jenny couldn't have made that up.

Tess read through the list of suspects and motives again, but no brilliant insight leaped out at her. She tore off the sheet she'd written on, stuffed it in the pocket of her robe, and went back downstairs without a book.

Sometime between 1 and 2 a.m., she finally fell asleep, and woke up again before six. She'd been having a bad dream, but it eluded her the moment she was awake. Knowing she would not be able to go back to sleep, she dressed in a warm red sweatsuit, heavy socks, and white athletic shoes. Last night, the TV weatherman had predicted temperatures in the teens today, and some of the rooms at the center were drafty.

She left the apartment and went to the big kitchen to make coffee. Then she got a pan of Gertie's cinnamon rolls from the freezer, removed the rolls to a plate, and defrosted them in the microwave. She squeezed oranges and half-filled a pitcher with the fresh juice.

She was putting the pitcher in the refrigerator when the memory of the dream that had awakened her surfaced. She'd been in the senior citizens center at night, terrified because somebody was chasing her. She couldn't find a door to let herself out, so she kept running in circles, while her pursuer gained on her. He was almost upon her when she'd snapped awake.

She closed the refrigerator door and leaned against it. No doubt Jenny's phone call had triggered the dream. Jenny had been alone at the center last night and she'd had the willies. Then she'd seen a car outside and had hung up. Had Ross come after the incriminating note

Jenny had found in the wastebasket? Had he intercepted Jenny as she slipped out the back door and headed for her car?

She was scaring herself with the possibilities. No doubt the police officer who checked on the center was right. Jenny had locked up and gone home without ever seeing who was in the car out front, but Tess wished now that she'd asked the police to check Jenny's house, too, to see if her car was there.

Glancing at the kitchen clock, she saw that it was just six-thirty. An hour and a half before the Hectors would be down for breakfast. Tess felt restless. She wanted to see Jenny and find out what, if anything, had happened last night after Jenny had hung up on her. She looked at the clock again. Jenny usually arrived at the center before seven to start preparations for lunch.

Quickly she scribbled a note for Milly and Skip, telling them to help themselves to coffee, juice, and cinnamon rolls, and anything else they found in the refrigerator that appealed to them.

She needed to drop off some things at the cleaners later, so she gathered them up to take with her — a wool skirt, two pairs of slacks, and two sweaters, but she couldn't find her black cardigan. She must have left it somewhere. She'd worry about the cardigan later.

She grabbed her coat and purse, along with the bundle of clothes for the cleaners, and left

Iris House. The red Honda parked at the curb reminded her that she hadn't heard Skip come in last night. He must have returned very late, after she was asleep. Maybe he'd been unable to sleep, too, and had decided to go back to Edwina's and sort through more of her belongings.

Possibly he had just wanted to be alone. Skip and Milly didn't seem to be getting along very well, and Tess wondered how much of that had to do with Edwina's death and Skip's reaction to it, as well as his reaction to Jenny Vercourt's sizable inheritance.

19

Tess parked in the graveled lot next to the center. Hers was the only car there, but Jenny and Willis usually parked on the other side beneath a carport attached to a storage shed.

She tried the front door first and found it locked. If Jenny was there, she'd be in the kitchen, too far away to hear a knock at the front door. Tess walked around the center, headed for a side door that led into a utility room and beyond that the kitchen. As she rounded the corner, she saw Jenny's car parked in the carport. She must have arrived just before Tess.

The side door was locked, too. Tess banged on it with a gloved fist and called Jenny's name. After waiting a couple of minutes, she still didn't hear anybody on the other side of the door. She knocked and called again. Still no response. She moved to the utility room window and peered in. There was no light in the kitchen.

Tess's anxiety returned stronger than before. She tried to console herself with the thought that Jenny's car wouldn't be there unless Jenny was there, too. Perhaps she was in her office. Pulling her coat collar up to protect her ears from the cold, Tess walked toward the carport, intending to circle around and try the back door.

She had reached the back of the building when she saw what appeared to be a tan boot beside the left rear wheel of Jenny's car. Alarm flooded through her as she ran forward.

Jenny Vercourt lay on the gravel of the carport, in the narrow space between the carport wall and her car. In jeans and a tan coat, she lay on her side, her arms extended toward the car, as though she were reaching for the black leather purse just beyond her fingertips. The purse's contents were strewn around it.

"Jenny!" Only when Tess knelt beside her could she see that the hair on the back of Jenny's head was matted with blood and her eyes were open, staring. Tess tore off a glove and felt for a pulse. There was none, and Jenny's skin was icy cold.

Tess got to her feet and ran for the apartments. The first apartment was unoccupied; Willis had been getting it ready to rent. Tess banged on the second door, Mercy Bates's apartment.

"Mercy! It's Tess Darcy. Open up."

She heard footsteps padding on soft soles, and the door cracked open. Mercy clutched a pink chenille robe closed with one hand. Tangled black curls framed her face, which was pale without her makeup, as she peered out at Tess. "Tess? I just got up. I'm not even dressed yet."

"Let me in, Mercy. I need to use your phone."

Mercy hesitated, frowning. Then, perhaps hearing the urgency in Tess's voice or recognizing in her expression the horror she felt, Mercy opened the door and let Tess in.

"What's wrong?" she cried as Tess brushed by her and went directly to the phone which hung on the wall in the kitchen. Tess knew the number of the police station by heart, but suddenly she could not bring it to mind. Shock, she supposed. "It's Jenny," she told Mercy. "She's been — hurt." She glanced down the list of emergency phone numbers Mercy had posted beside the phone, found the number, and dialed.

By the time the police arrived, Mercy had dressed and against Tess's advice followed her out to the carport, where she would have fainted on top of Jenny's body if Tess hadn't steadied her.

Chief Desmond Butts and Officer Andy Neill had secured the crime scene. Butts had gone out front to meet the ambulance and direct the attendants to the carport. Neill snapped pictures, then pulled on latex gloves and gathered up the contents of Jenny's purse, dropping them into evidence bags. Tess, who stood with Mercy just outside the carport, saw Neill try the car door and find it locked. Then he opened Jenny's wallet and looked inside. It was empty.

"Looks like robbery," he muttered.

The ambulance arrived, siren shrieking. Then Butts led two medics to the body. They maneuvered the corpse, stiff with rigor mortis, into a body bag. From what Tess had heard, the fact that rigor had set in meant Jenny had been dead for several hours. The medics carried her away on a litter.

The two policemen began conversing in low tones.

"Chief," Tess said, "could I talk to you in private?"

He had barely spoken to her since his arrival on the scene. Now he swept her with a distracted gaze before he said, "Neill, let me have that key ring. Must be a key to the center on there."

Neill handed over one of the evidence bags. Tess turned to Mercy and said, "You go on back to your apartment, Mercy. It's cold out here."

Mercy, who was huddled in an ancient fake fur coat, nodded dumbly.

"And don't talk to anybody," Butts barked as Mercy turned away.

Tess followed him to the back door of the center. He tried several keys before he got the one that opened the door. They stepped into the game room, where the seniors played cards and dominoes. The sun wasn't up yet and the room lay in shadow. Butts fumbled for a switch and turned on the lights.

He pulled out a chair at one of the card tables and jerked a hand toward the chair facing his, indicating that Tess should sit.

"They're dropping like flies around here," he growled. He shrugged off his leather jacket and ran both hands over his rough face. "I didn't even have time for a shave." He dropped his hands and scowled at Tess, as though that was her fault. "Neill says she'd been robbed."

"Whoever killed her might have taken the money to make it look like a robbery."

He scratched his beard-stubbled cheek. "Right. Seeing as how there's already been one murder at the center in the last week, I'm discounting the robbery theory for the time being."

"Oh, my God!" Tess gasped. "I just remembered. Somebody has to tell Jenny's husband."

"I'll send Neill by the house."

"Willis stayed in Springfield overnight. He may not be home yet."

"It's my job to worry about Willis Vercourt," Butts said pointedly. "Right now, you've got some explaining to do."

"About what?"

"For starters, do you usually get to the center this early?"

"No. Ordinarily I come about eight-thirty or nine. I came early today because I wanted to talk to Jenny. I was worried about her."

"Uh-huh." He eyed her narrowly. With dark beard stubble shadowing his cheeks and jaw, he looked like a Hollywood gangster. "Some kind of feminine intuition or what?"

Tess told him about Jenny's call the night before, about the car Jenny had seen in front of the center, the one she'd thought could be Ross's. She told him about her two calls to the police station. "The officer checked the front door. It was locked, and since there were no lights on and no car parked out front, he assumed Jenny had gone home."

Butts muttered an oath under his breath. "Must've been Rainey. He's so lazy he wouldn't yell for help if his clothes were on fire. I'll have a talk with that gentleman. He should've checked all the doors. If he'd come around back, he might have saved Jenny Vercourt's life."

Tess was relieved that his irritation seemed to have been transferred from her to Officer Rainey. Feeling a sudden rush of hot tears, she fumbled in her purse for a tissue and dabbed at her eyes. "I was upset by her phone call. I should have done more than call the police station. If I'd come and checked on her myself —"

"You're not on the force, Tess!" Butts barked. "Seems like I have to keep reminding you of that. If you'd come over here, you could've ended up dead, like Miz Vercourt."

She nodded, conceding the point. "Do you think whoever did this was waiting for her in the carport?"

"Maybe. Or the driver of that car she saw out front intercepted her."

"All that blood in her hair." Tess shivered. "He must have crushed her skull. What did he hit her with?"

"We haven't figured that out yet," Butts said. Which meant they hadn't found the weapon. "And I want you to keep your mouth shut about the blood and everything else you saw here this morning until the medical examiner gives us a cause of death."

Tess shivered again. The game room suddenly felt too cold. "When I got here, I found the front and side doors locked. I came around back to try the back door, and then I saw Jenny's car. I — I was actually relieved. I thought she had shut herself in her office and that's why she hadn't heard me knocking. Then I saw her boot."

"Did Miz Vercourt have any idea whose car she saw out front last night?"

"No. She couldn't see it very well. It was too dark."

"But she thought it was Ross Dellin?"

"She wondered if it was," Tess admitted. "We'd been talking about Ross and whether or not she should tell you about seeing him at Edwina's sewing box and about the note. I said

I thought she should."

"She didn't have the note on her," Butts said, shoving back his chair. "If the killer didn't take it, it's still around here somewhere."

"I think she was in her office when she called me. She said she had the note with her." Tess jumped up to follow Butts, who was already headed for Jenny's office.

After trying several keys from Jenny's ring, he found the one that opened the office door. He flipped on the light and walked to the desk, which was bare except for Jenny's notebook computer. Looking up, he saw Tess hovering in the doorway and said dismissively, "I can handle this."

She retreated to the kitchen, from where she heard him pulling out drawers and shuffling papers. After a while, he came out. "I checked everything. That note's not here."

"The murderer must have taken it."

"Tell me what it said again."

Tess repeated what she'd already told him. "Jenny was sure it was Edwina's handwriting. It was that part about the locker that made Jenny think it was meant for Ross."

"So what's his dirty little secret?"

Tess shook her head. "I don't know. Jenny asked him about it, but he said Edwina was a liar and threatened to sue Jenny if she told anybody the note was meant for him."

Butts frowned. "I didn't like Dellin the first time I talked to him. Where does he live?"

"On Queen Street in a yellow house across from the library."

Butts stomped out of the office and across the game room and opened the back door. "Neill!" he yelled, as he went out the door. "Go by the Vercourt house, see if you can find the husband. Then pick up Ross Dellin and bring him back here. I want to talk to him."

When Butts came back, he said, "I want you to hang around for a while. I may need to talk to you again."

"Somebody should be here when the seniors start to arrive anyway." There would be no lunch for the seniors today, but she could at least make coffee.

As she filled the coffeemaker with cold water and measured out the coffee, Tess tried to picture what had happened last night. Had it been Ross's car out front? Had Jenny let him in? Or had he, as Butts suggested, intercepted her in the carport? If he'd been there, it was to get the note. Perhaps Jenny had refused, and Ross's temper, which was never very far below the surface, had flared and he'd grabbed something and hit her.

If that's what had happened, Ross would have searched Jenny's person for the note. And ransacked her purse, throwing out the contents as he did so. If he hadn't found the note, he'd have used Jenny's keys to get into her office, then tossed the keys beneath her car with the items strewn from her purse.

Then he would have taken the bills from Jenny's wallet to make it look like a robbery and left, taking the murder weapon with him.

A scenario Tess could almost imagine. But it was a house of cards. There was no evidence that Ross had come to the center last night. The car Jenny saw could have belonged to somebody going to one of the houses nearby.

Had Jenny's death resulted from a simple robbery after all? Perhaps she'd refused to hand over her purse, had tried to fight the robber off. Or she might have recognized him. Even if he'd worn a mask, she could have recognized his voice. Perhaps she'd said his name, and then he'd killed her.

28

"Miz Vercourt was on the phone with Tess Darcy when you drove up at eleven o'clock last night." Butts was closeted with Ross Dellin in Jenny's office at the senior citizens center with the door closed. But Tess, who was in the kitchen next to the office, could hear every word he said, as the walls were thin and Butts made no attempt to moderate his tone. It was only seven-thirty, and none of the other seniors had arrived yet. When Officer Neill escorted Ross into the center, Tess had heard him report to Butts that Willis Vercourt had gotten back from Springfield only minutes before Neill arrived at the house. Vercourt assumed he'd just missed his wife and was leaving again to go to the center when Neill drove up. Willis had been so broken up by the news of his wife's murder that Neill had sat with him for several minutes before leaving to pick up Ross.

"You didn't know that, did you?" Butts demanded. Either he'd forgotten Tess's presence or he didn't care if Tess overheard his interrogation of Ross Dellin.

Ross mumbled something that Tess couldn't decipher. Risking being caught by Butts, she crept to the kitchen doorway, closer to the office.

"— the door locked," Ross was saying. "I thought she'd left, so I went back home."

So it had been Ross's car out front. "I was gone from the house less than ten minutes."

"Can anybody verify that?"

"No. I live alone." There was a pause during which neither man spoke. "A car passed the center as I walked back to my car," Ross continued. "If you could find the driver, he might have seen me knock at the front door and then leave."

"Can you describe the car?"

"It was a compact, I think. Looked like a two-door. Light-colored. Tan, maybe. It was dark. I can't say for sure."

"That's not much help, Dellin."

"Hell," Ross exploded, "if I'd been about to murder somebody, don't you think I'd have set up an alibi?"

"Maybe you didn't plan it. Maybe she refused to give you that note, and you killed her. By the way, what did you hit her with, Dellin?"

"I didn't kill her! I never even saw her!" Ross's voice was shrill with outrage. He stopped, as if to compose himself. Then in a lower tone, he said, "I admit I wanted that note."

"What made you think Miz Vercourt would

give it to you?"

"I didn't know if she would or not. I thought it was worth a try."

"So . . ." Butts drew out the word. "Edwina Riley was blackmailing you."

"No! I'm not even sure that note was written by Edwina. That's why I wanted to see it. I think I could recognize her handwriting. If you'd let me see it now —"

Butts ignored the suggestion. "What dirty little secret was she going to tell, Dellin?"

"Oh, crap," Ross groaned. "Why won't you believe me? I have no idea what Edwina or whoever wrote the note meant by that. And the part about the locker — maybe somebody was setting me up to look like Edwina's murderer."

"If Edwina wasn't blackmailing you," Butts demanded, "why'd you let her have that locker?"

"I decided it wasn't worth fighting over, so I gave her the damn locker. I thought that would be the end of it."

"Until Jenny Vercourt found the note."

"I didn't kill Jenny!"

"We'll get back to that. Why don't you tell me what you were doing at Edwina Riley's sewing box the day she died."

There was a long silence. Finally Butts said in a menacing tone, "You were seen, Dellin. So don't bother denying it."

"It seems silly now, but I found Mercy Bates's ring in the hall and decided to put it in

Edwina's box." Ross suddenly sounded very weary. "I knew Mercy would think Edwina had taken it and maybe raise a fuss. It was a way to get back at Edwina for her stubborn determination to have that locker."

"That sounds silly enough to be true, Dellin, from what I've heard about how you and Edwina Riley were fussing and fighting, but I thought you said you'd decided the locker wasn't worth fighting over."

"That was later." There was a long pause, then Ross added, "What does the ring have to do with anything? Why are you badgering me?"

"Look at it from my point of view, Dellin. Edwina Riley was blackmailing you and she's murdered. Jenny Vercourt had proof that Riley was blackmailing you and *she's* murdered. What would you think if you were in my shoes?"

"Wait! Wait just a damn minute here. I heard Edwina's needles were poisoned, and you know I was at her sewing box. You think I — You're trying to pin two murders on me! Well, you won't get away with it!"

"How did you know about the needles?"

"It's all over town. Now, I'm not saying another word. I demand to see a lawyer."

Butts mumbled something, and Tess barely had time to step back out of sight before Ross threw open the door of the office and barreled down the hall and out of the center.

Butts came out of the office. Tess walked casually into the game room and caught him looking pleased with himself. "He's gone to talk to his lawyer."

"Oh? Then I guess it was his car Jenny saw last night."

"He admitted it. Denied everything else, though." Butts turned to stare out a window. "As sure as I'm standing here, Dellin took that note," he mused. "It's probably ashes by now. And he's lying about not knowing what Edwina Riley had on him. Well, I'm not through with Dellin yet."

Tess kept silent, hoping he would go on talking. When he did, it was to say accusingly, "I thought I told you to keep the information about the needles quiet."

"I haven't told a soul," Tess retorted. "Maybe you should have a talk with your officers. The blabbermouth could be right under your nose."

He didn't pursue it but turned away, saying briskly, "You can go on home, Tess. I know where to find you if I need you."

"I'll just wait and see if any of the seniors show up so I can break the news about Jenny gently. Then I'll go home."

Butts shrugged. "Suit yourself," he said and left.

Tess poured a cup of coffee and sat at the kitchen table. From the way Butts looked when he came out of the office just now, Tess suspected he was already mentally outlining his case against Ross. Did Butts have enough to get an arrest warrant?

Tess didn't think so. The case against Ross was strictly circumstantial. Yet he appeared to be the only person who had a motive to kill both Edwina and Jenny. Despite Ross's denials, that note must have been meant for him, and now the note was gone. Which left Butts with nothing but Tess's hearsay evidence that the note ever existed.

As the seniors arrived at the center, Tess relayed the news of Jenny's death. Conscious of Butts's warning to keep her mouth shut about what she'd seen, she didn't even say it was murder. She said only that the police were investigating.

After talking amongst themselves for a few minutes, the seniors left. Tess had told them that she was going to lock up the center and she didn't know when Willis would feel like reopening.

Joyce Banaker lagged behind the others to ask Tess, "Where's Ross?"

"I don't know," Tess said honestly.

"I passed his car on my way here. He didn't see me. I don't think he was seeing anybody. He was red in the face, seething with anger."

"That's not too unusual for Ross. He's often angry about something."

"That's the truth! We could certainly do without him around here. Maybe he'll stop coming to the center now."

Tess looked at her in surprise. "I never thought Ross bothered you that much. He doesn't badger you the way he did Edwina."

"And the way he does Don Bob." Joyce's lips pressed together in distaste. "He ought to be flayed for the things he says to that poor man. All those sexual innuendos. It's a case of protesting too much, if you ask me. He's a dirty old man."

"Ross? Why do you say that?"

Joyce looked a bit startled, as if she'd said more than she'd intended. She waved a hand. "Oh, don't pay any attention to me. I'm so upset about Jenny."

"No, Joyce. If you know something about Ross, tell me. It could be important."

She shook her head. "I can't see how. I probably made it sound worse than it is. Perhaps many men indulge in pornography."

"Pornography! How do you know that?"

"A day or two before Edwina died, I was leaving the center and saw her in the parking lot, looking in Ross's car. She had her hands cupped at the sides of her face so she could see better. I stepped around the corner and waited for her to leave. I assumed her nephew was picking her up. She just stood there for a long time and then she went back into the center." Joyce looked faintly embarrassed. "Well, I was curious. So I looked in Ross's car before I left. There was a stack of girlie magazines on the back seat. One of them was open to a picture of a woman and two men —" She shuddered. "It was disgusting, Tess."

“My word.” But somehow Tess was not too surprised.

“Ever since then, when Ross makes some little dig at Don Bob, I want to tell him to go drool over his pornography and leave decent people alone. It’s all I can do to keep my mouth shut.” She sighed. “To tell you the truth, Tess, I may not come back here myself. It just won’t be the same without Jenny.”

“No, it won’t be,” Tess agreed.

When Joyce had gone, Tess rinsed out the coffeepot and set it to drain in the sink. She put on her coat, and making sure the front door was locked, went out to her car.

Now that she knew what Ross’s dirty little secret was, she’d inform Butts. But first she was going to confront Ross.

21

Tess dropped off her cleaning on the way to Ross's house. As she did so, she realized that with the shock of finding Jenny and then having to tell the seniors what had happened, she had forgotten to look for her black cardigan at the center. But it hadn't been anywhere in plain sight, so perhaps she hadn't left it there after all.

She parked in front of Ross's house and sat in her car for a moment, gathering her courage before going up to the house.

Ross's expression was grim when he jerked open his front door. "What do you want?" he demanded.

Hoping to take him by surprise, Tess plunged right in. "I know about the dirty little secret that Edwina discovered and tried to blackmail you with, Ross."

"You don't know anything!" He didn't invite her in, which was just as well. Tess didn't want to be alone in his house with him.

"Really, Ross. Pornography? At your age?"

"How did you —" He halted. Through the

screen door, Tess saw his hands clench into fists at his sides.

"Edwina saw pornographic magazines in your car and used that to make you give up the argument about the locker."

He folded his sweatered arms across his chest. He was cold, standing in the open doorway without a coat. "I suppose she told you that!" he snarled.

"No. Joyce Banaker told me. She saw the magazines, too."

He glared at her. Then he thrust out his chin. "Sounds like the whole damn bunch at the center paraded past my car for a look-see. Gave 'em a thrill, I guess. Well, so what? It's a harmless pastime for a harmless old man. It's not against the law, either."

"Not unless you're trafficking in pornography."

"Now, see here! You can get sued for slander!"

"Never mind threatening me, Ross. Either you go to the police and tell them about the magazines and Edwina's blackmail, or I will."

He stared at her, his eyes slits. "Somebody ought to teach you to mind your own business."

Tess took a step back from the door. "Like somebody taught Edwina — and Jenny?"

Color drained from his face and he reached out with both hands. For an instant, Tess thought he was reaching for her, and she took another step back, bracing to run if he opened the screen door. But instead he gripped both sides of the doorframe until his knuckles were white. "You don't actually believe I killed those women, do you, Tess?"

"I don't know, Ross, but you went to the center last night to get that note."

"Yeah. I never should've thrown it in the trash, but I figured Jenny would dump the contents without looking at them. Anyway, I admitted to the police that I was there. But nobody came to the door, so I left. I never saw Jenny or the note last night. That's the God's truth, Tess. I swear it."

"Then why is the note missing?"

His eyes widened. "It's missing? But Butts said — Or maybe I just assumed that he had it."

Tess hesitated, then tried to backtrack. "I could be wrong. Maybe Butts does have the note."

He studied her face. "If they didn't find the note, then there isn't much evidence against me, is there? Even with the note, my lawyer says they can't arrest me on what they have."

"You and your lawyer can't know what evidence Butts has. I certainly don't."

He stared at her. "And you're still going to the police?"

"I'll wait a couple of hours," Tess said, "to give you a chance to go yourself. Do it, Ross. It'll be better if it comes from you."

A bitter laugh escaped him. "Like I got an attack of conscience or something?" He lowered his head and shook it, as if trying to fling off the vision of Tess standing on his porch and practically accusing him of murder. "Look, I despised Edwina Riley, Tess. She was like some kind of noxious weed, spreading poison to everything she touched, but I didn't kill her. I let her have the locker and hoped that would be the end of her threats. If she'd tried to blackmail me again, I was prepared to tell her to go ahead and broadcast that she'd been nosing around my car and seen some girlie magazines. Hell, that wouldn't have ruined me."

That was true, Tess had to admit. But if the word had got out, it might have been embarrassing for Ross.

"I'm not hypocritical enough to say I'm sorry Edwina's gone," he was saying. "But for God's sake, I'll miss Jenny. I would not have harmed a hair on that woman's head."

He dropped his hands and his shoulders sagged. His face was gray; he suddenly looked very old.

Ross sounded sincere, but was he? At the moment, he merely looked depressed, almost beaten. "Tell it to the police, Ross," Tess said finally, turning away.

She heard the door close as she got into her car.

A few flakes of snow drifted against her windshield as Tess drove to Cinny's bookshop.

Cinny was seated on a stool at the cash register counter, poring over an interior decorating magazine.

"It's starting to snow," Tess announced as she breezed in.

"Great," said Cinny sourly. She closed the magazine and pushed it aside. "That'll be a boon to business."

"Still not selling many books, huh?"

"I had exactly five customers yesterday and one so far today," Cinny said. "She bought two paperbacks. Can't pay the rent on that."

"Business will pick up soon."

"Has to," Cinny observed. "Can't get any worse. You'd think this cold weather would make people want to sit inside with a good book. They must be sitting inside glued to television. Fortunately — if I can hold out another month — tourists are great book buyers."

Tess had no doubt that Cinny could hold out as long as necessary. If she got in a financial bind, her father would bail her out.

Desperate to talk to somebody, Tess asked, "Have you heard about Jenny Vercourt?"

"Jenny? No, what about her?"

Ignoring Butts's voice, which echoed in her head telling her to keep her mouth shut, Tess swore Cinny to secrecy, then told her everything. Within a day or two, the whole town would know anyway.

Cinny was stunned. "I can't believe it! You think it was one of those old people who come to the center who killed her?"

Tess shook her head. "Haven't a clue."

"Which one could it possibly be?" Cinny continued. "Mercy Bates? Joyce Banaker? Don Bob Earling? It boggles the mind. Ross Dellin is the only one I can even imagine doing it."

"When I went to Ross's house earlier, I was convinced it was him," Tess said, "but when I left I wasn't so certain."

"He sure gets my vote," Cinny said. "I'll tell you one thing. I may abandon the book discussions. I'm not sure I want to go into that place again. Are you going back, Tess?"

"I don't know. I'll talk to Willis in a week or two. By that time, February will be almost over anyway."

"Do you think Willis will want to keep the center open?"

"I imagine so. The center and the apartments provide a decent income. But Jenny was the glue that held it all together. It certainly won't be the same without her. For one thing, keeping the apartments repaired is pretty much a full-time job. Willis can't take on all that Jenny did, too. If he keeps the center open, he'll have to hire someone to help him."

"This is so awful for him," Cinny murmured. "Does he have much family around here?"

"I don't think so. There aren't any children, and the only relative I ever heard Jenny or Willis mention is Willis's sister in Springfield.

Maybe she can come and stay with him for a few days."

Cinny walked around the counter and to the front of the bookshop. "The snow has stopped, but the sky is ugly. Looks like it could start snowing again any time. What a horrible month for a funeral." She turned back to Tess. "I can't help thinking about Jenny. If only she hadn't gone back to the center to work last night."

Tess went to stand beside her and study the sky, but the weather was the least of her concerns. "I keep thinking about Ross," she said. "He sounded so sincere when he swore he never saw Jenny or the blackmail note last night."

"Then what happened to the note?"

"That's the question, isn't it?"

"This conversation is getting morbid," Cinny said with a sigh.

"Then let's change the subject. I didn't leave my black cardigan here, did I?"

Cinny shook her head. "Haven't seen it."

"Well, it's not in my apartment, so I hope it's at the center." Chewing her bottom lip thoughtfully, Tess watched the owner of the antique shop across the street arranging a new display in her window. "Darn, I hate to lose that sweater. It's one of my favorites."

"It'll turn up," Cinny said. She sighed again as she surveyed her full bookshelves. "Let's lock up the shop and go somewhere for lunch."

Tess agreed readily. She didn't really want to

be alone until she was sure the police knew everything about Ross that she did. Until then, she wasn't certain she'd feel quite safe in her apartment.

After lunch, Tess phoned Chief Butts from the bookshop to ask if Ross had come to see him.

"Dellin was here. Other than that I can't say. I don't care to discuss police business with a civilian," Butts retorted curtly.

"He swears that he never saw that note," Tess said.

"All murderers lie," Butts snapped. "They'll even lie when telling the truth is easier and might actually help them. It's in their genes. Now, if you'll excuse me, Tess. I have work to do."

She was listening to the dial tone. She replaced the receiver, irritated by Butts's attitude. He'd evidently decided she was no more use to him in the investigation, so he was shutting her out.

"That man is enough to make *me* commit murder," she groused to Cinny.

"Mr. Personality he's not," Cinny agreed.

Tess left Cinny alone in the bookshop and went home, looking forward to spending the evening with Luke.

22

After Tess returned to Iris House, Luke called to say he had to cancel dinner. An out-of-town client had arrived and wanted to go over his investments. As Tess ate a sandwich in her kitchen, she heard Skip and Milly arguing upstairs. What was said was too muffled to decipher, except when Skip yelled, "I thought you'd gotten over that crazy notion!"

The exact nature of the crazy notion, Tess was not to know, for she could not make out Milly's reply.

A half-hour later, Milly appeared at Tess's apartment door with her suitcase. "I'm checking out," she announced.

Tess invited her in. "Let me get your statement, and I'll give you a receipt." When she returned to the sitting room with the bill, Milly was seated on the sofa. In response to the invasion of a stranger on her turf, Primrose had vacated her chair and disappeared.

Milly signed the credit card form and handed it to Tess.

"Is Skip going back to Fort Worth with

you?" Tess asked.

Milly shook her head. "Nope. He'll be staying in Edwina's house until it's sold. He's packing right now. I offered to wait and drive him over there, but he said he'd walk." She grimaced. "He's being a martyr, but it won't kill him to walk a few blocks with his suitcase."

"Where will he go when he leaves Victoria Springs?"

"I'd be the last to know."

All at once, Tess realized she was close to tears. "Are you all right, Milly?"

Milly blinked hard a few times and made a face. "I'm fine. It's just — Well, Skip and I had a falling out and I told him I didn't want to marry him and he could find somewhere else to live if he returns to Fort Worth."

"It's late for you to be starting on such a long drive."

"I didn't exactly plan it this way, but I couldn't stay with Skip another night."

"I'm sorry, Milly," Tess said.

Milly lifted her shoulders. "Don't be. Almost from the moment we arrived in Victoria Springs, I realized it wasn't going to work. I can't live with somebody I can't trust. Skip says I'm the one who's changed. Maybe he's right. I just know that I don't feel about him the way I used to."

"I heard you arguing a while ago," Tess admitted.

"Then I guess you heard Skip blow a fuse

when I asked if he happened to be anywhere near the senior citizens center last night when Jenny Vercourt was murdered."

So that was the crazy notion that made Skip yell at her. "I knew he went somewhere late last night," Tess said. "I assumed he'd gone over to Edwina's to do more sorting and cleaning up."

"That's what he told me. He said he couldn't sleep, so he thought he might as well do something useful."

"You don't believe him?"

Milly lifted both hands in a gesture of futility. "The problem is I'm having trouble believing anything Skip says lately. And to tell you the truth, I'm not sure why, but I never know what he's thinking anymore."

Tess sat down in a side chair and said earnestly, "Milly, do you think Skip had something to do with Jenny's death?"

"Probably not," she said. "It's just that he was furious about her getting the inheritance from Edwina. I guess three-quarters of a million isn't enough for him. He wanted it all. I'm only now learning how greedy Skip is."

"But what would killing Jenny accomplish? Surely he understands he still won't get her share of the inheritance."

"I suppose," she mused.

"Milly, would you mind my asking you a few things about Edwina and Skip?"

"I guess not."

"Were they close?"

"Not at all. I've been with Skip for almost two years now, and we've lived together for ten months. He rarely mentioned her name until he decided we should visit her."

"Did Skip know he was mentioned in Edwina's will?"

"Oh, sure. She told him he was her heir. He assumed he was the only heir until we got here and Edwina told him she'd left something to a few other people. She didn't give him any details, but it bugged him."

"Did Skip have any idea that Edwina had such a large estate?"

Milly hesitated. "He swears up and down that he didn't. He knew she owned the house and he thought she probably had five or ten thousand dollars in a savings account." She looked pensive for a moment, then seemed to shake herself and stood up. "Tess, I'd better get started. By the way, I love Iris House. It's the one bright spot in the entire visit for me. I appreciate your letting us stay here."

Tess followed her to the door. "Come back any time."

"Thanks, but I'll never set foot in this town again. Too many bad memories." She picked up her suitcase, which she'd left just outside the door. "Tess, you're right about Skip. He had no motive to kill Jenny Vercourt. It's just — this whole thing has made me crazy. I can't wait to get back home to a normal life again."

Tess closed the door and leaned back against

it, aware of the fact that in spite of what Milly said, she was suspicious that Skip was involved in Edwina's murder, if not Jenny's. Skip's inheritance gave an out-of-work young man a powerful motive for murder if he'd known the size of the estate Edwina had accumulated. Even though he'd sworn to Milly that he hadn't known, Skip was, as Milly had said herself, an accomplished liar.

The night before Edwina's death, Tess had found Skip sitting alone at the kitchen table. How long had he sat there after she'd gone back to her apartment? A suspicion that she'd had before came back to her. Skip could have had the kitchen to himself for the rest of the night, if he'd wanted. Plenty of time to cook up a batch of poison.

There had been no evidence the next morning that anyone had used the stove, but then Skip would have been careful to clean it thoroughly and any pots he might have used.

After making sure the dead bolt was thrown, Tess wandered back to her office. She'd straighten her desk, clean out her file cabinet, do anything to keep herself from conjuring up any more frightening scenarios. As with Ross Dellin, there was no real evidence against Skip for either of the murders. And the fact that the blackmail note Edwina wrote to Ross had been taken would seem to eliminate Skip as a suspect — for Jenny's murder, at any rate.

Nevertheless, a half-hour later, she was glad

when she heard Skip leaving. She ran upstairs to make sure he'd left all the keys to Iris House. The keys lay on top of the dresser.

Tess breathed a sigh of relief, finally able to admit to herself that she hadn't wanted to be alone in the house with Skip. Everything but the fact that the blackmail note meant for Ross Dellin was missing seemed to point to Skip as the murderer of two women. Did the missing note really clear Skip? Tess didn't know.

She sat down at her desk and turned on her computer. Luke had given her the computer for Christmas and had helped her learn the basics she needed to write and print out letters and to maneuver through the bookkeeping program he'd installed. She had to admit it was better than the ledger where she'd formerly posted income and expenses by hand.

She pulled up the bookkeeping program and took several bills and receipts from a desk drawer to post. It didn't take long. When she finished, she logged off and moved to the window seat, where Primrose was napping. The Persian stretched, yawned, and cuddled up next to Tess, who scratched behind her ears. The sound of the cat's contented purring filled the room.

It was getting dark. The yard lamps, equipped with electric eyes, flashed on as she sat, staring into the gloomy shadows, thinking about Jenny's funeral tomorrow at the Presbyterian church.

The sanctuary would be full. Jenny and Willis were well liked around town. At lunch today, everybody in the restaurant had been talking about Jenny's murder. Several people had come by Tess and Cinny's table to express concern over Tess's state of mind, since she'd been the one to find the body. They'd also wanted to know if she was aware of anything about the murder that they hadn't yet heard. Tess had pleaded ignorance of what the police might know and what they were doing about it.

Tomorrow those people as well as Tess would be at the funeral to say good-bye to Jenny.

23

The next afternoon, Tess and Luke squeezed into a back pew in the already full sanctuary of the Presbyterian church. They'd barely made it in time because Luke had had a last-minute long distance call from one of his clients. The Dow Jones industrial average had plunged seventy points the day before, and the client was panicking. Luke managed to calm him down, but it had taken ten minutes.

Organ music filled the sanctuary and as soon as Tess and Luke were seated, the minister took his place on the podium. Then a woman who was hidden behind a screen, began to sing "Rock of Ages," her voice beautifully rich and full of feeling. Luke reached for Tess's hand and squeezed gently.

Tess saw Joyce Banaker, the Bloom sisters, and the McBrooms seated together a few rows in front of her and Luke. Don Bob Earling was there, too, at the end of the pew midway in the section to Tess's right. Ross Dellin sat behind and to the right of Don Bob, his head bowed. She didn't see Willis, who was seated in the front row, until the brief service ended and the family members left the sanctuary. An attractive blond woman clung to his arm as they came down the aisle. They were followed by an older couple whose faces were scored by devastating grief. Jenny's parents, Tess surmised. Various other relatives followed the couple.

Since it was not an open-casket service, the congregation was ushered from their pews to the foyer row by row. Seated in the last row, Tess and Luke were among the first to leave the church. Jenny's relatives had formed a line in the foyer to accept condolences.

Willis appeared to have aged ten years since Jenny's death. His face was gray, the lines on either side of his mouth etched deeper than Tess remembered. Her heart went out to him. Hugging him, she whispered, "I'm so very sorry, Willis. What can I do to help?"

"Your just being here is more than enough," Willis said haltingly, as if it was an effort to push the words out. Tess took a step back and looked into his bleak eyes. "Thank you for coming. Jenny was very fond of you."

"And I her," Tess said. "Are you sure I can't do something, Willis?" She was conscious of the line of people waiting behind her.

Willis studied her face for a moment. "If you really want to, you can come to the center and help me pack." At Tess's startled look, he added, "I can't keep it going without Jenny,

Tess. She was the motor that kept everything running."

"I know," Tess sighed. "But do you think you should make such a major decision so soon after losing her?"

"I won't feel any different a month from now — a year from now. And the sooner I can sell the property, the better. Until then, I won't be able to go on with my life — what's left of it."

"Then I'll be glad to help you pack whenever you're ready."

"I'll be there tomorrow afternoon. I have to keep busy, keep my mind on something besides . . ." His voice trailed off.

The poor man was rudderless. In spite of Tess's misgivings about his closing down the center so quickly, she promised to be there the next day.

Willis introduced her to the blond woman, his sister from Springfield, and the older couple from Kansas City. They weren't Jenny's parents, as Tess had surmised, they were her foster parents. Jenny's parents had died when she was a young teenager. Tess and Luke moved on down the line, introducing themselves and murmuring sympathy to various nephews, nieces, and cousins, all of them from out of town.

Wordlessly they left the church and walked to Luke's Jaguar. As Luke drove out of the parking lot, Tess said, "I hope Willis doesn't regret his decision to close the center. I've always heard you shouldn't make those kinds of decisions right after the death of a spouse."

"Generally that's true," Luke said. "But Willis is right about Jenny being the mainstay of that operation. Opening the center was her idea, and I seem to recall that Willis had his doubts about it in the beginning."

"I know he worked long hours keeping up with repairs," Tess said. "He couldn't continue with that and do everything that Jenny did, too. I suppose I assumed he'd hire somebody to help him. The center provides a lot of needed services."

"We'll discuss it at the next chamber meeting," Luke said. "The board will want to do something about finding another way to offer the services. We can probably get local churches involved."

As promised, Tess arrived at the center at two o'clock the next afternoon. Finding the front door unlocked, she opened it and yelled, "Yoo hoo! Willis!"

"Coming."

He appeared in the rec room a few minutes later carrying a pair of scissors and a roll of packing tape. His denim shirt was rumpled, and there were streaks of dirt on his wrinkled khaki trousers. Beard stubble darkened his cheeks and chin, and he looked exhausted.

Tess stepped into the rec room. "How long have you been working here?"

"A couple of hours. I didn't realize there was so much to pack."

Tess took off her coat and hung it with her purse on the corner rack. "I can't find my black cardigan sweater. Have you run across it?"

"No, but I've had my mind on other things. You can look around."

"Okay. Now, tell me what you want me to do."

"Come on back to the game room." She followed him down the hall past the lockers, many of which contained books, sewing boxes, and other things.

"One thing I could do," Tess suggested, "is call the seniors who've left things in the lockers and let them know when they can reclaim their belongings."

They'd reached the game room, where empty cardboard boxes of various sizes were stacked on the floor. "Would you, Tess?" Willis asked. "I hadn't even thought about that stuff in the lockers. Tell them I'll be here today and most of tomorrow if they want to come by. I don't know what to do about that quilt in the sewing room."

"I'll see if the McBrooms can take possession of it. The quilting is almost finished anyway. I think they could finish it with a hoop in their apartment."

"Good." He sighed heavily and indicated eight or nine boxes he'd already filled and sealed with tape. "I'm going to rent a storage unit for this stuff until I figure out what to do with it. Do you think you could tackle the kitchen? I'm still hauling stuff down from the attic. I left a stack of newspapers on the kitchen table for packing the dishes."

"Sure." Tess dragged a couple of boxes into the kitchen and got started. Willis went back to the sewing room, where there was a pull-down ladder for entering the attic. Soon Tess heard his muffled footsteps overhead. She worked for an hour, packing dishes, pots and pans, and small appliances. It made her sad to think of all of the things Jenny had accumulated here banished to a storage shed. But Willis would have no use for them now, and perhaps he'd donate them to a worthy organization. As she was getting the broom and dustpan from the broom closet, she found her sweater. It hung on a hook at the back of the closet. Jenny must have put it there, intending to tell Tess she'd found it. Tess took the sweater to the rec room to hang it on the rack with her coat and purse. As she did so, something rattled in a pocket. She thrust her hand in and pulled out a folded piece of paper. She opened it. It was Edwina's blackmail note to Ross.

Frowning, Tess refolded the note. Now how had it gotten into her sweater pocket? Perhaps Jenny had put the sweater on the night she was killed. Tess recalled her saying that the center was chilly. The sweater must have been lying somewhere handy, and Jenny put it on, removing it when she was ready to go home, stuffing the note in the sweater pocket until she could turn it over to the police. Now Tess would see that Butts got the note.

Still pondering, she walked slowly back down the hall. The note's still being in the center seemed to be a point in Ross's favor. Would he have killed Jenny without first getting the note? She didn't think so. Which left Skip Hector as the strongest suspect in both murders.

Tess went to the foot of the stairs and called up to Willis. "I've finished in the kitchen. Do you want me to empty Jenny's desk and file cabinet?"

His head appeared in the opening as he wiped his dusty face with a handkerchief. "Please," he said. "Just be sure to label the boxes. You're a godsend, Tess. I can't thank you enough."

"Don't mention it." Returning to the game room, she grabbed a box and took it into Jenny's office. She'd clear out the office, then call the seniors to tell them to pick up their things.

She set the notebook computer into the box, then began emptying the file cabinet. By the time she'd packed the files, the box was full. She sealed it, wrote Computer and File Cabinet Contents on the side with a Magic Marker she'd found in the kitchen, and got another box for the contents of the desk.

She pulled out the center desk drawer and

scooped up paper clips and pens and pencils, dropping them into the empty box.

As she pulled open another drawer, she had a flash of memory. She could see Jenny seated at her desk with her computer, inputting figures, trying to find the money to remodel the center's kitchen. When Tess had come in, Jenny closed the computer and put the pages from which she'd been copying figures into an envelope. Then she'd bent down and put the envelope in a hidden compartment she pulled out from under the desk. She'd sworn Tess to secrecy, saying that it was her secret hiding place and nobody else knew about it.

Tess knelt down and bent to look under the desk. And there it was, a metal tray no more than an inch and a half deep, centered and flush with the underside of the desk. She crawled into the kneehole and felt around until she found a small protrusion. It moved to one side when she pressed it, and she could then pull the tray out.

She set it on the desk and lifted an envelope from the tray. Inside, several pages of figures were folded together — the notes Jenny had been using at the computer that day she told Tess about the secret compartment. Tess put them aside also and took out the last sheaf of papers contained in the drawer. The pages were legal-sized, folded once, and when Tess opened them, she realized that what she held was Jenny's copy of Edwina Riley's will.

She was about to put the will aside as well when the printed letterhead at the top of the first page caught her eye: *March, Walker, Herschel and Fillbrook, Attorneys-at-Law.* She had a duplicate copy of the will at home, of course, but she'd never paid any particular attention to the letterhead before. Now she did. Something about it niggled at her. She read it aloud and then she knew what was bothering her.

Willis's sister was a paralegal who'd recently changed jobs, according to Jenny. Formerly, Jenny had said, she'd worked for a firm with a long name. *March, Walker, Something, Something.* Willis's sister had worked for the firm of Jason Fillbrook, Edwina's attorney.

Suddenly Willis loomed in the doorway. "You about through here?" Tess had leafed through the will to the last page and read the date, less than two years prior to Edwina's death. Jenny had said that Willis's sister had changed jobs only recently, which meant she had worked for Fillbrook's firm when Edwina made her will, had surely had access to all the firm's files, and must have known that her sister-in-law stood to inherit a considerable sum of money upon Edwina's death.

"Your sister worked for Jason Fillbrook, Edwina's attorney," Tess blurted out. Only then did everything fall into place in her mind, too late to call back the words. And far too late for Edwina and Jenny. She pushed back her chair and stood, the will still clutched in her hand. Tess had never been any good at poker; her face always gave her away.

Willis did not move from the doorway. His gaze dropped to the will in Tess's hand, then came back to her face, and his expression changed.

Her only option was to try to carry it off. "Yes, I'm finished here," she said brightly. Too brightly.

At the same moment, she heard faintly the creak of the center's front door. Tess prayed that the man before her, the man she'd thought was grieving over Jenny's death, was so focused on her that he hadn't heard.

She stepped toward the door, but Willis didn't move to let her pass. "How did you know my sister worked for Fillbrook's firm?"

Trying to be offhand about it — and failing miserably, she was sure — Tess moved behind the desk chair so to put it between herself and Willis. She said clearly and distinctly, and she hoped loudly enough for whoever had entered the center to hear, "Jenny told me, but at the time she didn't know that Edwina's lawyer was part of that firm. Only you knew that, because your sister told you that Jenny was one of Edwina's heirs."

He had sinister eyes. Why had she never noticed that before? "Don't say anymore, Tess." It was a jagged whisper.

But she'd said too much already. "She had

access to all of Fillbrook's files. So of course she told you how much Jenny's inheritance would be. But you couldn't wait for Edwina to die a natural death. She could have lived for another twenty years, and you needed the money right away. Does your sister know that you murdered Edwina Riley?"

He took a single step, and Tess gripped the back of the chair.

"Leave my sister out of this! She knows nothing!"

Perhaps he was telling the truth. Tess couldn't tell. She no longer trusted her instincts where Willis Vercourt was concerned. "Did Jenny find out what you'd done?" Tess shook her head in disdain. She lifted her voice. "Is that why you killed her?" She allowed herself one brief glance over Willis's shoulder. Had she imagined hearing the front door? If somebody had come in, where was he?

"Shut up, Tess!"

They stood there, frozen in a terrible tableau. What was Willis willing to do to shut her up? Tess began to tremble. Whatever it took, she guessed. Willis had already killed two women, so he would hardly balk at a third. Tess imagined Butts calling on Luke and Aunt Dahlia and Cinny to tell them he'd found Tess's body. The thought almost closed her throat and made her voice raspy. "Did you want the money so badly, Willis?"

"I wanted it for both of us." His voice shook.

"I wanted to sell the center, take the money, and retire. You can't know how sick I am of trying to keep this place up. We could have lived off the income it generated, not lavishly, but well enough. And Edwina had no use for it. She wouldn't even paint her house!"

"But once Jenny had the inheritance, she wouldn't go along with selling the center."

"She wanted to put it all into this place, like throwing the money down a rat hole. We argued and argued, and I went to Springfield just to get away and cool off."

Tess remembered that Ross Dellin had seen a light-colored compact car the night Jenny was killed. "But you came back that night, and not in your car. You must have borrowed your sister's."

"I told you my sister knows nothing about any of this! The car was rented. I just wanted to talk to Jenny again. I never meant to hurt her." Yet it must have been at the back of his mind as a last resort, or else why take such pains to make sure nobody saw his car in Victoria Springs that night?

"I found her here, but she wouldn't listen to reason," Willis said. "She turned her back on me and walked out of the center. She said she was going home and she didn't want to talk about the money anymore."

"You followed her and struck her down. Left her body lying there on the dirt and drove back to Springfield. Came back home the next morning when Officer Neill told you your wife had been murdered. Did you feel even the slightest tinge of remorse?"

"Of course I did! I don't know how it happened. I didn't mean . . . I lost my temper." He lowered his head, shook it like a large animal shaking off a blow. Then he lifted both hands and came toward her. "Nobody knows but you."

Frantically Tess pushed the chair forward, jamming it into Willis's legs. He stumbled back. "You'll never get away with it, Willis!" She was almost screaming now. "Luke knows I'm working here with you today. And — and I called Chief Butts to tell him I'd found the blackmail note Edwina sent to Ross. The Chief should be here any minute."

He studied her for a long moment. "You're lying!" He skirted the chair and made a lunge for her. Tess staggered back and screamed.

At last footsteps approached, and Ross Dellin clumped into the office. "What the hell's going on in here?"

Willis's head jerked around and he bolted, shoving Ross aside.

"Stop him, Ross!" Tess yelled. "He's the murderer!"

Lowering his head, Ross thundered across the game room like a great, lumbering bull, grabbed Willis at the back door, and brought him down. Tess would never forget the sound of Willis hitting the floor front first, like a felled tree. Before he could get to his feet again, Ross had grabbed a chair from one of the game tables and brought it down on Willis's head. Ross stood over him, panting, the chair raised to strike again if he moved. But Ross didn't have to worry. Willis was out cold. Blood oozed from a cut on the side of his head.

"There," Ross gasped. "That oughta hold him till the police get here."

"I'll call them," Tess said, darting back into the office.

"I heard you tell Willis you already did," Ross called after her.

"I lied," Tess said. "And by the way, it took you long enough to show yourself!"

24

It was mid-morning the following Thursday when Tess dropped in on Cinny at the bookshop. She had picked up a copy of the local weekly newspaper from the box outside the shop and glanced at the photograph of herself with Ross Dellin which ran with the lead article's headline: LOCAL RESIDENTS CATCH KILLER.

Later she might read the article, which occupied about half the front page, just to see if the editor had gotten the quotes right.

Two other stories took up the rest of the front page, one about Skip Hector, the other an interview with Chief Butts. As Tess entered the shop, she scanned the story about Skip, "the heir to a near-million dollars," who was living in Edwina's house until it sold and was, reportedly, still grieving for his late aunt.

Cinny was shelving a shipment of new books. Seeing Tess, she grinned. "You made the front page, cuz."

Tess waved her paper. "I noticed."

"Have you read the interview with Chief Butts yet?"

"No." Tess tossed the paper on the cash register counter and went behind it to pour herself a cup of coffee.

"He says he already suspected Willis Vercourt and was about to interrogate him when he got your call that Willis had confessed. I don't believe it for a minute."

"Oh, well. Whatever makes him feel good."

Cinny slid the last book from the carton at her feet onto a shelf, then carried the box to the back and tossed it into the storeroom. Coming back, she eyed her cousin carefully. "How are you holding up?"

"I'm fine — thanks to Ross."

Cinny laughed. "Good old Ross. How did he happen to show up at the perfect moment?"

"Pure coincidence. Or maybe ESP. While I was packing up everything in Jenny's office, I was thinking that as soon as I finished, I had to call him and the other seniors and tell them to come by the center and pick up their belongings. I also wanted to tell Ross that I'd found the blackmail note and would turn it over to the police. Meanwhile, Ross was just driving by, saw my car, and came in to find out what the status of the center was."

"Your guardian angel was working overtime."

"You bet." Tess settled on one of the two stools behind the counter, her coffee mug in both hands. "And Mercy called me yesterday. She finally got Wally Tanksley to tell her what

Edwina told him."

"Which was?"

"That Mercy was going all over town saying that she and Wally were getting married. Mercy told him that Edwina lied, but she's not sure Wally believed her. He's still steering clear of Mercy."

"That's too bad." Cinny shook her head sadly.

"Maybe he'll come around," Tess said hopefully.

After a moment, Cinny asked, "Do you know what will happen to Jenny's share of Edwina's estate?"

"According to Butts, it'll go to her closest relatives, a niece and nephew in Washington state."

Cinny sobered. "Cody says Willis could get the death penalty."

Tess didn't want to think about that. She sipped her coffee. "So how's business?"

Cinny shrugged. "It's picked up a little this week. I'll be so glad when the tourists start arriving and I can afford to hire an assistant again. You want to have lunch in town today?"

"Sure. We might as well enjoy this idle time. Come March, I'll have a full house. This week, though, I've been making plans. In fact, that's the main reason I came by."

"What sort of plans?"

"For my wedding — and I'd like you to be a bridesmaid."

Cinny let out a whoop and grabbed her, almost causing her to spill what was left of her coffee. "You finally set the date!"

Extricating herself from Cinny's arms, Tess set her mug on the counter. "June fifteenth. I've already phoned Dad and they can make it then. The whole family will come over from Paris. Maddie will be my maid of honor. I think Luke is going to ask his assistant, Sidney Lawson, to be best man, and he mentioned Cody and Curt as groomsmen. And of course I want Aunt Dahlia to take charge of organizing the wedding and reception."

She went on to tell Cinny about the addition to Iris House. The workmen were scheduled to start on it the first of March.

Cinny folded her arms and beamed at Tess. "This is great! Honestly, I thought you would vacillate over a date and where you and Luke would live for at least a year. No wonder Luke's been looking so happy lately."

They spent the next hour talking over the wedding plans. Finally Cinny giggled and said, "This is going to give Mother ideas about Cody and me."

"Speaking of Cody and you —"

Cinny held up her hand. "No, Tess. We haven't gotten that far yet."

"Hmmm. The way you phrased that, sounds like you might get that far in the near future."

Cinny merely smiled and bent down to retrieve her purse from beneath the counter. "It's only eleven, but let's lock up and go buy something special to celebrate. You'll need a trousseau."

"There's plenty of time for that."

But Cinny was already putting on her coat. "Come on, Tess. It'll be fun!"

Sighing, Tess followed her cousin from the shop. Shopping with Cinny was like following a whirlwind around while trying to stay out of its path. It was exhausting, even exhilarating, but Tess wouldn't exactly call it fun.

Still, by the time they were in Tess's car and headed for Cinny's favorite dress shop, Tess had begun to catch her cousin's excitement. Cinny did have a good eye for fashion.

Tess glanced at Cinny and smiled. Not for the first time, she gave silent thanks to her late Aunt Iris, who'd left her Iris House, for making it possible for Tess to move to Victoria Springs. It was nice to walk down the street and hear people say, "That's Frank Darcy's daughter, and Dahlia Forrest is her aunt."

Sometimes being so close to family could feel restricting. But most of the time, like now, it was pleasant and somehow comforting.

Iris House Recipes

Tess's Potato Casserole

2 pounds frozen hash brown potatoes, thawed
1 cup sour cream
1 can cream of potato soup
1 can cream of celery soup
1/3 cup chopped onion

Mix all ingredients in 9×13-inch Pyrex dish and bake at 350 degrees for 1 hour.

Anita's Broccoli and Raisin Salad

1/2 cup mayonnaise
3 tablespoons balsamic vinegar
1/3 cup sugar
3 cups broccoli flowerets, raw
1 cup raisins
8 to 10 slices bacon, cooked crisp and crumbled
1/4 cup chopped green onions

Mix all ingredients and chill before serving.

MERCY'S BAKED SQUASH

5 pounds medium yellow squash
2 eggs
1 1/2 cups bread crumbs
4 ounces butter
1/4 cup sugar
2 teaspoons salt
2 tablespoons chopped onion
Dash pepper

Cut off squash tips. Cut squash in 3 or 4 pieces. Cover with water and cook till tender. Drain.

Mash squash and add eggs, 1 cup bread crumbs, butter, sugar, salt, onion, and pepper. Place in 2-quart baking dish. Cover with the rest of the bread crumbs. Bake at 350 degrees till lightly browned.

Don Bob's Chicken Salad

2 tablespoons lemon juice
2 1/2 cups diced cooked chicken
1/2 cup diced celery
1/4 cup chopped onion
1 teaspoon salt
1/4 teaspoon pepper
1 tablespoon chopped pimento
3 tablespoons chopped walnuts
1/3 cup mayonnaise
1/2 cup seedless green grapes
1/2 cup drained crushed pineapple

Pour lemon juice over chicken. Add celery, onion, salt, pepper, pimento, walnuts, mayonnaise, grapes, and pineapple. Mix thoroughly. Chill before serving.

HATTIE'S DINNER ROLLS

1 package yeast
1 cup lukewarm water
1/2 cup shortening
1/2 cup sugar
1 cup hot mashed potatoes
1 cup hot potato water
2 teaspoons salt
1 egg, beaten
6 to 6 1/2 cups flour

Mix shortening, sugar, potatoes, and potato water. Cool to lukewarm. Dissolve yeast in cup lukewarm water. Add to above mixture. Cover. Let stand in warm place till light and bubbly (about 2 hours). Add salt, egg, and flour to make a stiff dough. Cover. Store in refrigerator for at least 24 hours. The dough may need to be punched down once or twice until it's cool.

With greased hands, pinch off walnut-sized pieces of dough and place 3 in each cup of well-greased muffin tins. Let rise until more than double in size before baking. Bake at 425 degrees for 15 to 20 minutes. The dough may be kept in refrigerator for 4 to 5 days and baked as needed.

Opal's Ham Casserole

1 cup cooked diced ham
1/4 cup green pepper cut in 1-inch strips
1/4 pound mushrooms, quartered
Dash thyme
2 tablespoons butter or margarine
1 10 1/2-ounce can cream of chicken soup
1/2 cup water
2 cups cooked rice
1 9-ounce package frozen artichoke hearts, drained
2 tablespoons sherry
2 tablespoons chopped pimento
1/4 cup shredded Cheddar cheese

Brown ham in skillet (no oil needed), turning until all sides are browned. Drain off any accumulated grease and set aside. Cook mushrooms, green pepper, and thyme in butter until pepper is tender. Combine mushroom mixture, soup, water, rice, artichokes, sherry, pimento, and ham in a 1 1/2-quart casserole. Sprinkle cheese on top. Bake at 350 degrees for 30 minutes.

VICTORIA SPRINGS BAKERY'S CHOCOLATE CREAM CHEESE BARS

1 cup sugar
3 8-ounce packages cream cheese, softened at room temperature
5 eggs
2 teaspoons vanilla
1 tablespoon lemon juice
1 4-ounce package sweet baking chocolate, melted and cooled

In mixing bowl, combine sugar and cream cheese. Beat until fluffy. Beat in eggs one at a time. Add vanilla.

In a separate bowl, measure 2 cups of the cheese mixture; fold in chocolate and set aside.

Add lemon juice to remaining cheese mixture and pour into a well-buttered 9-inch square pan. Top with chocolate mixture and swirl slightly with a knife to marbelize. Bake at 350 degrees for 40 to 45 minutes. Cool, then chill. Cut into bars.

We hope you have enjoyed this Large Print book. Other G.K. Hall & Co. or Chivers Press Large Print books are available at your library or directly from the publishers.

For more information about current and upcoming titles, please call or write, without obligation, to:

Publisher
G.K. Hall & Co.
295 Kennedy Memorial Drive
Waterville, ME 04901
Tel. (800) 223-1244
(800) 223-6121

OR

Chivers Press Limited
Windsor Bridge Road
Bath BA2 3AX
England
Tel. (0225) 335336

All our Large Print titles are designed for easy reading, and all our books are made to last.